The Flight
of the
Shadow Drummer

Paul Travers

Duncan & Duncan, Inc., Publishers

The Flight of the Shadow Drummer

For information or to contact the author, address correspondence to:

Duncan & Duncan, Inc., Publishers
2809 Pulaski Highway
Edgewood, MD 21040
410-538-5580

Library of Congress Catalog Card Number: 97-69496

Travers, Paul, 1951—
    The Flight of the Shadow Drummer

ISBN: 1-878647-44-X

10 9 8 7 6 5 4 3 2 1

Dedication

To Catherine, the heart and soul of the Shadow Drummer.

To Cynthia and Deborah, the new generation of shadow drummers who sounds the call for peace and freedom.

Table of Contents

Chapter One—

Life on the Plantation

Thunder boomed across the Chesapeake Bay like cannonade from a distant battlefield. High above, rain clouds trampled across the bright, blue sky. Down below, whitecaps churned the surface in a boiling caldron of silver and green. A howling wind signaled the attack was beginning. Ping! Ping-Ping! Ping-Ping-Ping! Raindrops fell like bullets. As the storm approached land, it picked up speed for its final assault. The grey curtain of water loomed larger and larger.

From the heavens, the boy on the shoreline appeared as a black speck. Moses stood at the water's edge with his hands outstretched and his toes buried in the wet, grainy sand. He watched in awe as the forces of nature waged another of their endless battles.

Within seconds, Moses was surrounded by the battle. As the rain splashed his face, he opened his mouth to dampen his parched tongue. He licked his lips and savored every drop of the cold water. But Moses knew the feeling was temporary. No matter how long the storm raged, the rain would never seep into his soul. Deep inside his heart, a searing fire burned with a white heat which could never be extinguished.

Lightning stabbed the ground in every direction. The blinding flashes signaled a retreat. With the wind at his back, Moses turned and ran. He quickly settled into a rhythmic trance, moving to the cadence of a pounding heart and pulsating lungs. Like a frightened deer, he leaped over fallen logs and darted around trees. Here in the forest, he was alone with his thoughts and free from the plantation. He ran hard because he wanted to think hard. His mind always raced as quickly as his feet. He wanted to think about his future. But he knew that no matter how far he ran, he could never leave his past or catch up with his future. At times like this, his inner thoughts were as dark and stormy as the weather.

Catching his breath, Moses stopped at a small pond in a cluster of scrawny pine trees. Leaning over the edge, he stared intently at his reflection. Then like a clown auditioning for the circus, he started a routine of funny faces. He pulled his eyes, twisted his nose and squeezed his cheeks in an attempt to laugh at himself. The faces were more grotesque than humorous, so he stopped.

Once again, he stared at his reflection. The effect was hypnotic. Ever so slowly, he raised his hands to his head and gently swept his fingers along his face. All faces were the same; eyes, ears, nose, lips and teeth. Moses realized how similar he was to his owner, Master Steele. Indeed, they were the same except for the color of their skin. Color was the only difference between master and slave, yet Master Steele owned the slaves and the slaves owned nothing, not even their faces.

The dark thoughts he had tried to outrun had caught up with him. "What right does one person have to own another?" Moses asked himself. Lately, this disturbing question often came to mind. He tried to ignore it, but it snuck up when he least expected. Part of growing up, he reasoned. He was sure every slave thought the same at one time but never dared to speak. Why should he have these thoughts, Moses pondered. He had a good life on the plantation. There were family, friends, food and a house. What more could a person want in life? Perhaps, this business about master and slave was the natural order of the world, and he had no right to even think about it, much less question it. Then again, perhaps it was not.

Leaping over a row of thorns, Moses landed ankle-deep in the mud of the freshly plowed tobacco field. As he neared the cluster of ramshackle log cabins, he pumped his arms in a furious sprint to the first dwelling. Slowing to a trot, he noticed the field slaves huddled in the doorways, waiting for the storm to pass. Seeing them look forlornly at the sky brought a mischievous grin to his face. It was a fact of life that slaves feared the crack of lightning more than the crack of the whip. He remembered the rage of Master Steele when three slaves and an ox were killed by a bolt of lightning.

"Damn lightning," Steele cursed. "I can always buy me three lazy Negroes, but it's not everyday I can buy me a hard working ox."

"True enough, boss," said Hunt, the plantation overseer who constantly courted the favor of his boss. "But at least you can eat what's left of the ox and let them Negroes fertilize the field."

No slave laughed at the morbid humor on that day, but they did have the last laugh. There was something to be gained by this particular misfortune. For a week, there was red meat for supper. The god of the master and the god of the slave certainly worked in mysterious ways, Moses thought.

When Joseph heard the horn, the signal for the slaves to halt work, he closed the blacksmith shop and hurried home to tell his wife the latest news.

"Good Lord, Martha! It's hotter than a hundred hells in here," he bellowed as he swung open the rickety cabin door.

"And the devil himself just came home," Martha replied as she stood huddled over the fireplace. "No one knows heat better than you."

"The devil's own doorman, dressed in fire and smoke," Joseph squealed with delight. "Why I bet under this suit of soot, my skin is chalky white, the same as Miss Lizzy. Why, we may even be family."

"You old fool," Martha chastised. "Master Steele better not hear you talking like that or he'll tear that fine suit off of your back with a bullwhip."

"Wouldn't that be a fine sight to see," Joseph mused, rubbing his chin. "A white devil whipping a black devil. Wonder whose side Satan would take?"

Joseph lumbered wearily across the room and pulled up a chair next to Martha. "Where's Moses?" he asked somberly. "Better not be running around with that crazy Luther. That boy's nothing but trouble. He's either too smart or too dumb to know he's just a slave like the rest of us."

"Now watch what you say about Luther," Martha cautioned. "Once you said you admired his courage."

Joseph grunted in agreement and watched as Martha tended the fire. Her shadow danced around the scraps of furniture scattered about the room. He wondered where her frail body found strength. After washing, sewing and cooking for the Steele family, she did the same for her own. It must be that religion, he thought. Martha was a righteous woman who believed mightily in the Bible. Somewhere in that book, she found the courage to persevere. Those Old Testament words must cast a magic spell on the person who recites them, Joseph reckoned. Of all the slaves he had known, his wife was the only one who was allowed to read. Every evening before bedtime, she read a Bible story to Master Steele's children. Even for a slave, there was some good in the good book. For Martha's sake, Joseph hoped the Bible made no distinction between slave and master when it came to believing.

Moses pulled open the squeaky door and cautiously peered inside.

"Just the person I need to see," Joseph declared. "I've got good news. Master Steele said you're too old to be a houseboy; no more women and children. Starting tomorrow, you'll be the new stable boy. Luther will teach you all you need to know before he goes to the field."

Moses nodded his head and headed for the door without a word. His heart raced and his head spun from the news. Standing outside in the rain, he felt two feet taller. At last, he was taking his rightful place on the plantation. At age twelve, he had passed into manhood.

Early the next morning Moses followed his father to work. Passing the orchard, his nose caught the sweet fragrance of the apple trees. A hundred yards later, his nostrils filled with the pungent odor of hay and horse manure. Directly ahead loomed the stable. The stone building with an overhanging slate roof was the hub of activity on the plantation. Every plantation visitor passed through its doors. As a result, the stable boy held a position of power among the slaves. He was their eyes and ears to the outside world.

Luther stood outside leaning on his pitchfork. In this early hour, he was well into his workday. Joseph made brief introductions and quickly departed, but Moses needed no introduction to this gangly sixteen year old man-child. Luther's exploits were the talk of the plantation. Whether they were fact or fiction mattered little to the slaves. To them, he was a strange paradox, a rebellious slave who somehow incurred the favor of his master.

At times, he provided comic relief to their dreary existence. Whenever he vanished for more than a few hours, rumors about his latest escape spread like wildfire. In a carnival atmosphere, slaves bet contraband tobacco and liquor on his capture. At other times, he was a troubling reflection of their lives. Deep inside their hearts, they harbored Luther's courage. They desperately wanted to escape the plantation but were afraid to take the first step. They silently cheered whenever there was a rumor of his disappearance.

"Stable boy is a good job," Luther stated earnestly. "Do it right and it will keep you out of the fields. Do it wrong and you'll die in the fields. Take good care of Master Steele's horses, and Master Steele will take good care of you."

"Yes, master. I'll do everything you say and more," Moses replied in a comical tone, trying to ease the awkwardness of the situation.

"Don't worry. I'll teach you a thing or two about master and slave," Luther muttered under his breath, obviously unimpressed by the joke.

From the outset, Moses wondered how good of a teacher Luther would be. After all, he was Luther's replacement so Luther could work the fields. No slave wanted to work the fields. Walking up and down the rows of tobacco plants was a long, slow, painful journey to the graveyard. Moses was stuck. He had no other teacher and no other choice. He knew absolutely nothing about horses. A bad teacher was better than no teacher at all.

For the next few weeks, Moses shadowed his instructor and studied his every move. If he was to survive as the stable boy, he had to keep his eyes open and his mouth shut. Luther's success as Master Steele's jockey in the summer races was no fluke. Luther was an equine expert. He knew everything about horses. Better than that, he knew everything there was to know about Master Steele's horses.

Moses quickly discovered that taking his place on the plantation was easier said than done. Stable work was an endless and exhausting routine of cleaning, feeding and grooming. Muscles ached constantly from pitching hay and mucking out stalls. The only break came when Luther worked with the horses. Every afternoon, he exercised them in the pasture next to the stable. Moses sat on the fence and marveled at Luther's horsemanship as he led each horse through a series of walks and gallops. With a whisper of his voice, a tug on the reins, or a slap of his hand, the horses were at his command. Moses knew Luther was an outstanding teacher. He wondered if he was going to be an outstanding student.

Home for Moses was now the hayloft which he shared with Luther. Living space was cramped but comfortable. Compared to the cabins in shantytown, the loft was a luxury hotel. A pile of hay and a thick horse blanket made for a good bed and a good night's sleep.

Despite their uneasy friendship, Luther rarely talked. He spent late nights in the tack room, cleaning and polishing leather. He seemed more than content to be alone. Moses, on the other hand, needed Luther, but Luther was always gone. Moses was panicking. He needed information and needed it fast. He still had hundreds of unanswered questions. In another week, the apprenticeship was over, and he would be on his own.

One night after making a final check of the horses, Moses was surprised to find Luther sitting atop one of the bales. "Eureka!" he mumbled under his breath. This was the golden opportunity he had been waiting for. But mining gold in this hayloft was not going to be easy. Luther's scowl put him on guard. Moses was afraid to speak much less ask a question.

"It's time for your final test," Luther commanded.

"But I still need to learn a few things," Moses stammered nervously.

"I don't mean that kind of test. I mean the test of life," Luther replied curtly.

Moses swallowed hard and said nothing. He waited for Luther to make the next move.

"Bet you're wondering why I don't talk to you much," Luther said.

"Never really gave it much thought," Moses replied casually. He didn't dare let Luther know his silence troubled him.

"Don't know if you can be trusted?"

"Trusted with what? I know everything about the stable. In another week, you'll be out in the fields and I'll be in charge. I'll do just fine."

"I don't mean the stable. I mean trusted with the secrets of the plantation. I know everything about this place. I think you might want to know them, but only if you can be trusted."

"Cross my heart and hope to die," Moses said nervously, wondering what he was getting himself into.

Luther accepted the oath with a nod and began his story.

"My real name is Katumbe Katumba, son of an African warrior. One day while hunting, my father and I were captured. We sailed across the ocean in the belly of a ship, chained with hundreds of sick and dying slaves. We arrived in Annapolis, just across the bay, where we were auctioned. Before we separated, I promised my father I would return home to care for the family. Two years ago, I made my escape. Early one morning, I got up and just ran away. I lived off of the land, eating berries and roots. After two weeks of crossing marshes and rivers, I reached the edge of the great ocean. The water stretched to the sky. Waves as tall as trees crashed on the beach. I knew my home was on the other side, thousands of miles away. I started to build a raft, but was captured by bounty hunters before I could finish. They brought me back to collect their money. That's when Master Steele said runaways needed to be taught a lesson."

Luther's rapid fire delivery suddenly stopped. Tears welled in his eyes.

"And then what happened?" Moses blurted out, no longer able to contain his excitement.

Luther leaned forward and stiffened like a statue. He stared straight ahead without blinking an eye. Sweat beaded on his brow and rolled down his cheeks.

"And that's when Mister Hunt cut off my big toe," shrieked Luther as he kicked off his shoe. Moses recoiled in horror at the sight of the deformed foot. "Said next time he'll chop off my foot. Your mother nursed me until I got well. Why, Master Steele was so afraid his prized stable boy was going to die from the fever, he gave me horse medicine. It worked. I'm alive and well. Now, all I want to eat are hay and oats."

Luther slapped his thighs and laughed madly at his joke. He waved his foot high in the air so Moses could get a closer look at the missing toe. "That was the end of my dream. And before I tell any more secrets, tell me, Moses. What is your dream?"

The question caught Moses by surprise. "I don't know," he mumbled as Luther's eyes burned through his soul. "Never really had much time to think about it." From the look on Luther's face, he knew that was the wrong answer.

"You know all about Luther the horse boy. Now tell me something about Moses the houseboy," Luther growled.

Moses thought for a moment. "A drummer!" he cried out. "I want to be a drummer boy in the army."

"Somebody better wake you up! You certainly are dreaming," Luther howled with laughter. "But at least you have a dream. That's important. You see, the problem with the slaves around here is that they lost their dreams; buried them in the fields. My job is to help them find it. That's why I must go."

"And just what is their dream?" Moses asked.

"Freedom!" Luther shouted defiantly.

"Of course, freedom. I should have known," gulped Moses. The sound of the word made him wince. He immediately remembered the stormy day at the beach and the haunting thoughts about master and slave.

"Know anything about drumming?" Luther asked sincerely, hoping to restore his friend's confidence.

"Not too much. Once in a while I see the militia in town. Occasionally, Colonel Steele tells me a war story," replied Moses, shaking his head sideways.

"Just like I figured, nothing." Luther placed his hand on his chin and raised his eyes to the rafters. "You know this old horse boy might be able to help you, but you have to keep a secret."

Moses was puzzled. "I thought you just told me your secret."

"That was only part of it. Some secrets have no ending, but don't worry. The best is yet to come, now that you can be trusted."

That night Moses closed his eyes and imagined Luther's escape. How could a slave find his way to the ocean, he wondered.

Where did he go and who did he meet on his journey? A buried treasure came to mind. Master Steele often talked about Blackbeard the Pirate who plundered villages along the Chesapeake. Maybe, that's the secret. Luther found the buried treasure and would buy his freedom.

Moses thought again. Maybe his imagination was getting the best of him. That night, he dreamed he saw Luther running one step ahead of a razor-edged cutlass, brandished by a swarthy figure sporting an eye patch and a bandanna. Clink! Clink! Gold doubloons rolled on the ground as they spilled from Luther's sack.

The next morning Moses tried to solve the mystery of Luther's escape. More disturbing than his story was his talk about freedom. After seeing Luther's foot, Moses knew escape for him was out of the question. Life as the stable boy was good. He wasn't going to throw it away on some harebrained scheme of a deranged slave.

Luther refused to say anymore about the secret. After a few days, Moses decided the story was a hoax and stopped his nagging questions. It was as if their conversation never took place. In the evenings, Luther was his moody and brooding self. Instead of spending time in the tack room, he was preoccupied with studying the heavens. As the full-moon approached, he sat by the window for hours and stared at the stars. Once again, Moses was totally ignored and more than puzzled.

Chapter Two—

The Secret of the Medicine Man

Luther shot three quick jabs to Moses' shoulder. "Wake up!" he whispered. More nonsense about the moon, Moses thought as he rubbed the sleep from his eyes. "Time to discover the secret."

"Right behind you," Moses exclaimed as he cast aside his blanket and scampered down the ladder.

The plantation glowed in the dull, bluish light of the full moon. Chimney smoke from the shanties coated the air with a whitish haze. Despite the eerie brightness, it was difficult to see clearly. Silhouettes and shadows blended with one another into total darkness.

Luther certainly knew what he was doing. It was light enough to see, but not light enough to be seen. Holding his finger to his lips, he crept along the stable wall. When he reached the corner of the building, he executed a series of turns and leaps before disappearing into the trees. Moses mimicked the moonlight ballet as closely as possible.

"Where are we going?" he asked as he caught up with Luther.

"To the woods," Luther replied.

"We're already in the woods. How far in the woods are we going?" Moses shot back impatiently. He feared Luther was escaping. Quite possibly, he was being suckered into the plan as a decoy.

"About two hours. Hurry, we haven't a second to spare."

Without another word, Luther dashed into the forest. Despite a severe limp, he trotted at a brisk pace which had Moses panting for air after a few minutes. Luther floated like a ghost. In the moonlight, his cocoa skin melted into the night, making him nearly invisible. He moved quietly and confidently as if he had made the journey a thousand times.

To keep up the pace, Moses lengthened his stride. His legs ached and his lungs burned. Sweat ran freely down his face. The thought of bounty hunters supplied a burst of energy and fought the fatigue. He could feel the axe's sharp edge cutting into his foot. Being away from the plantation was risky business, but he found the danger thrilling. If this was a taste of freedom, perhaps, he could understand Luther's voracious appetite.

Luther finally stopped for rest. Moses dropped to his knees and asked the question which had been weighing him down.

"Are we escaping?"

"No," came the bullet response. "I told you I ain't getting caught a second time. So leave it at that."

Luther's eyes burned like hot coals. He acted like a man possessed by a demon. He stared into the night as if his eyes were beacons that could penetrate the darkness. Despite a good hour of running, his face was dry and clammy; not a bead of perspiration anywhere on his body.

The pair sprinted across an open field and stopped at the edge of another forest. Here the pine trees soared to the heavens like cathedral spires. Luther grabbed Moses by the hand and led him forward. Step by step, they stalked a point of light which flickered in the distance.

"We're here," whispered Luther. "This is the secret."

Moses looked around in disbelief. A campfire was ablaze in the middle of the forest, and not a soul was in sight. Some secret, he thought. Before he could utter a word, a voice came from the shadows on the other side of the fire.

"Good to see you again, Katumbe. I see you brought a friend this time."

Luther pushed Moses in the direction of the voice. "Moses, I would like you to meet Patayac, shaman of the Nanticoke Indian nation," he said proudly.

Moses slowly extended his hand which was quickly grasped by the tall stranger who emerged from the shadows. In the trembling light, Moses saw the copper, almost reddish, tan of the man's skin. Staring down at him was a long, weathered face, crisscrossed with wrinkles. Strands of long, black hair rested on the man's shoulders.

Patayac was dressed in pants and a vest made from animal hides. His feet were covered in moccasins. Moses had never seen such a sight. On rare occasions, a defiant slave wore pieces of homemade native garb to incur the wrath of Master Steele, but nothing compared to the stranger's costume.

"Tonight we come as brothers. Tonight we remember," Patayac said in a deep, comforting voice. His smiling eyes sparkled with a hypnotic energy as he motioned Luther and Moses to sit.

For the next hour, Luther and Moses listened keenly to the Indian's tales. He talked about his tribe who lived between the great bay and the great ocean. Once upon a time, fields were covered with corn, beans, pumpkins and tobacco; forests were filled with deer, turkey, rabbit and squirrel; and the great "shell-fish bay" was teeming with fish, crabs, clams and oysters. Life was good in a land of plenty.

But Patayac's tale had a tragic ending. For befriending the white man, his people were forced from their land to reservations where they died off one by one. As the last member of his tribe, it was his sacred duty to bless the land which marked the final resting place for many of his people. For three days, he prayed and fasted to cleanse his spirit. He hoped for a vision of the future which would predict the return of his people to their land.

"Why do you come to remember?" Moses asked Patayac after he had finished his story.

"I am the last of my tribe. I recite the history of my people to the mother earth so she will remember. The wind carries my voice across the universe. The trees, rivers and the rocks listen. They may be silent for thousands of years, but one day, they will recall the story of my people."

"But will it matter to the rest of the world if your people are forgotten?"

"It matters for my people, your people and all the people of the world," replied Patayac. "People are like trees. They need strong roots to survive in the forest. By remembering our roots, we will be strong. Not only will we understand our own people, but we will understand others around us. Our future is locked in our past."

"Does that mean the white man, the red man, and the black man will one day live in peace?" Moses asked.

"A simple question with a very difficult answer, Moses. You see the white man has forgotten his roots. He no longer lives in harmony with nature. Look around! The forests are thinning, the rivers are drying up, and the animals are disappearing. What the white man doesn't understand, he ignores, or worse yet, he destroys. There is room for all men on this planet."

"But will there ever be . . . "

"Enough questions for one night, my friend. The hour is late." Patayac turned to Moses and clenched his hand. "Remember, Moses. My people like your people were taken from their land. We are children of the sun, tribal people who live in harmony with nature. One day when the white man shares that harmony, our people will return and prosper. Go quickly! Your captors will be angry if you are missing."

Back in the loft, Moses pondered the night's visit. It was an unbelievable journey he would remember forever. He often heard the older slaves talk about strange noises in the night, but, until tonight, they were only ghost stories. Now he knew the truth. He understood why Luther was so guarded about his secret. Patayac would be hunted down like a runaway slave for trespassing on his own land.

The secret was out, but that didn't explain everything about Luther. The more Moses thought about Patayac's predicament, the more confused he became. What did the Indian have to do with Luther? Moses closed his eyes and wrestled with the question for what seemed an eternity. The stories of Luther and Patayac mingled in his mind. Images of Luther running through the forest and Patayac living off the land danced in his head. As if struck by lightning, he bolted upright. "He helped you escape," he shouted at Luther. But Luther was fast asleep, lost somewhere in his own dreams. Moses chided himself on his stupidity. The answer was obvious from the beginning. No man alive knew more about the land and water than Patayac. How else could a slave survive?

The next night Luther and Moses retraced their steps. When

they reached the campfire, a fierce looking Indian stood before them. Patayac's face and arms were streaked with red and white paint. His head was shaved on both sides, leaving a spiked strip in the center of his scalp. A cape of feathers was draped over his shoulders. Around his neck hung a necklace of eagle claws and animal teeth.

Luther and Moses sat with Patayac in front of the fire. After minutes of silence, Patayac slowly lifted a long-stemmed, wood pipe, adorned with feathers, and held it high above his head. "Tonight we honor Manito, the god of all good. We ask him to bless this sacred ground which holds my ancestors. Let us share this pipe as a sign of peace."

Following Luther's lead, Moses inhaled deeply. He eyes bulged and his throat burned as the hot smoke collected in his lungs. Gasping for air, he coughed up a cloud of thick, white smoke which hung around his head like a halo. It felt as if someone had set his lungs on fire. After the pipe had been passed, Patayac started the conversation.

"Luther tells me you want to be drummer," Patayac said to Moses.

"That is my dream," Moses whispered meekly.

"It is good to dream. Every man must have a dream. Now, you must follow your dream. If you don't, it will disappear like a cloud in the sky. Be warned. The road you follow will be dangerous, but the rewards will be many."

"Will we have time to talk tonight?" Moses asked. "You didn't have time to answer my questions last night."

"Tonight and many more nights we will talk, but first there is something more important I must do."

Moses spied the hand drum and rattle on the ground next to the fire. "Are you a drummer?" he asked.

"No. I only use the drum to call on my brother the eagle who carries my prayers to the sun. The white man thinks the Indian is a child who worships the sun and the moon. But we worship nature no more than the white man worships the pictures inside his stone churches. We worship the spirit behind the sun, the creator who gives life to the universe. My church is here under the moon and the stars," Patayac said, waving his hand across the sky.

Moses and Luther stood alongside Patayac in front of the fire. "Tonight is special. Tonight you are welcomed into my tribe as brothers," Patayac proclaimed joyously.

He placed his hands on each boy's shoulders and said a prayer in his native tongue. Taking a white paste made from clay, he marked their foreheads with a cross inside a circle. "The earth is your mother who has given you roots. She will always remember who you were during your life," he intoned gravely.

Plucking a feather from his vest, he dusted their faces. "One day your spirits will soar with the eagle. From the heavens, you will witness the majesty of the universe."

Luther and Moses threw handfuls of corn husks and tobacco leaves on the fire and sat down. Patayac, picking up the drum and the rattle, began the ceremonial dance. Swish! Thump! Swish-thump! Swish-thump! Raising the rattle high over his head and slapping the drum against his side, he hopped and skipped around the fire.

"Aye-ya-na-hah! Nay-he-yah-nah!" he mumbled in strange words. His voice fluctuated between a deep bass and a shrill falsetto with each repetition. He slowly increased the tempo of his singing and playing until it reached a feverish pitch. He smacked the drum with the rattle like a thunderclap. His chant was now a piercing wail. Flames leaped into the air as he sprinkled a magical powder on the fire. White smoke swirled in a dizzying spiral. Caught up in the excitement, Luther and Moses jumped to their feet and danced in place. Patayac sprinted madly around the fire, his arms and legs a blur. Suddenly, he fell to his knees as if he had been shot.

"No, Manito! No, Manito!" he cried out in agony before falling face down in the dirt.

Luther rushed to his side and gently cradled his head.

"I have seen my vision," Patayac gasped with a look of horror on his face. "I saw thousands of hands reaching for me from the spirit world. My people have passed into history. They will never return to their land. Now, I must join them as the last warrior."

"He's dead," screamed a stunned Luther.

"What are we going to do?" asked a frightened Moses.

"We must finish the ritual so his spirit will reach the heavens," Luther insisted

He picked up the drum and rattle and danced wildly around the fire, mimicking the steps of Patayac. Tears streamed down his face. After a few circles, he stopped and threw the drum and rattle into the fire. "A sacrifice to Manito!" he shouted. The dry wood hissed and sizzled before bursting into a brilliant blue flame.

"Do you think we have freed his spirit?" Moses asked nervously.

"We did the best we could," Luther lamented. "Hopefully, by the time we reach the plantation, Patayac will be walking with Manito next to the great shellfish bay."

Using large, flat stones, Luther and Moses carved out a shallow grave for the medicine man and marked his final resting place with his peace pipe. They doused the dying fire and hurried home. Luther led the way. He ran as fast as his feet could carry him. Moses kept the pace, a step behind all the way without a complaint. He knew the feeling. Luther was trying to distance himself from Patayac's death.

At the edge of the woods, they stopped to rest. Both boys fell on their hands and knees, sucking in air. After a minute of deep breathing, they were revived. As they slowly stood, the leaves in the trees rustled. They froze in place. The noise moved directly overhead. Luther expected bounty hunters to drop from the branches. Moses' eyes bulged from their sockets, and his mouth hung open. He was sure this escapade would cost him a toe. Suddenly, an angular silhouette drifted across the sky. Silently and swiftly, the owl soared to the heavens. Patayac was riding the night wind to the home of his ancestors.

In the loft, Luther sobbed softly for a few minutes, then fell into a deep sleep. Moses, too excited to even close his eyes, went outside for some fresh air. After tonight, he needed time to clear his head. It had been a night to remember for eternity. Looking up at the moon and the stars, he pondered Patayac's words of wisdom. A gentle smile creased his face. "Patayac, I know you can hear me," he whispered softly. "Tonight, I promise you that I will follow my dream."

Chapter Three—

Riders on the Storm

Morning broke wet and gray over the plantation. A storm front moved in overnight and stalled. It looked like the plantation would receive a thorough soaking over the next couple of days. Fortunately for Moses, Luther's disposition was not as grim as the weather. With the death of his best friend still fresh in his mind, Luther was upbeat and rather cheerful. He laughed with Moses as they watched the slaves slip and slid in the mud on their way to the fields. Patayac died, the rain fell, and life went on without missing a beat.

"The weather is a good omen. Manito must be pleased. Right now, Patayac splashes about in his great shellfish bay and baptizes us with his holy water," Luther proclaimed.

"I believe you're right," Moses chimed in. "These raindrops are tears of joy, not tears of sorrow."

The rest of the morning passed in silence. Luther busied himself with his work. He pitched straw like a machine, pile after pile without a break. A glaze of perspiration covered his body like a film of oil. Occasionally, Moses glanced over, ready to cue on Luther's conversation. He hoped Luther would start talking about Patayac. He was sure it would ease his troubled mind.

Late in the morning, the stable had its first visitor of the day. Footsteps rapidly approached. Even before the stranger came into sight, his identity was revealed. The rhythmic pounding of boot heels on the cobblestone signaled the alarm. Mr. Hunt was in the area. As usual, Luther and Moses were ready for his grand entrance.

"Just the boy I need to see," growled Hunt, standing face to face with Luther, his chin only inches away from Luther's. "To-morrow you're in the fields with the rest of your kind. You'll be sleeping in the cabins. The stable is for the stable boy only. I'll see you in the fields at sunrise." Hunt spit on the ground in disgust and headed out.

After a few steps, he spun around and pointed at Luther. "I'm going to find out right quick just how much thoroughbred is in you," he roared with a menacing glare. "You're no longer Steele's jockey. This time I'm the jockey. I'm going to ride you long and hard, and I'm not afraid to use the whip. And remember one thing, don't you dare spook and run on me."

When Hunt was gone, a bewildered Moses looked at Luther. He had often heard Hunt rant and rave in a temper tantrum, but he had never seen this dark, threatening side. "Aren't you afraid?" he asked.

"Don't have to be afraid, just careful. He's as evil as the devil himself, but he's no fool. He'll never do anything to the stable boy as long as Steele's horses are well-cared for. Don't worry about me. I'll deal with him on his own terms."

Luther's false bravado was an act. He tried to convince him-self he was as fearless as any man, but deep inside he was wor-ried. Hunt's words were more than a dare. They were an invite to challenge his authority. Luther took comfort in the fact he would never face the challenge. A greater one was calling him, and its voice grew louder with each passing hour.

That night in the loft, Luther wiled away the evening by tell-ing stories about Patayac.

"I first met Patayac about two years ago on the night I de-cided to run away. It was so dark I just stumbled over him. At first, I thought it was a dead body. He didn't make a sound, not even a whimper. He was in a trance waiting for his vision. From then on, he treated me like a son. He taught me about the Chesa-peake Bay and the Atlantic Ocean. When I planned my escape, he told me to stay away from the ocean. But I was too foolish to listen. But now, I'm older and wiser. I'm sorry you didn't get to know him better."

"I would have liked that. I had many questions for him," said Moses, feigning a yawn. This was one night he needed to rest, even if it meant skipping some great stories. "I guess I should get to bed. Tomorrow's my first day as stable boy."

"Hey, Moses!" shouted Luther with a wide grin. "I'll stop by every evening. I promise."

"I'm going to miss you," Moses replied with a weak smile. "You're the best friend I ever had."

Luther grabbed Moses from behind in a bear hug. "Trust me. I won't let you down," he laughed as he lifted him off the floor. "But you're right. Let's get some sleep. Tomorrow's going to be a busy day for both of us."

Luther wrapped himself in his blanket and waited. He replayed his plan over and over. He was sure tonight was the right time. The death of Patayac and his encounter with Hunt only confirmed his decision.

When he was sure Moses was sound asleep, he rolled out of bed and fetched a leather bag hidden behind a bale of hay. Stepping lightly, he tiptoed to Moses. "Good-bye, my friend. Someday we will meet at the end of our dreams," he whispered as he kissed him on the cheek.

Once outside, he crouched against the stable wall. When the last candle in the manor house was snuffed, he moved toward the trees and vanished into the night. He turned around to take one last look at the plantation. The only thing he was leaving behind was his friendship with Moses. He was troubled about lying to Moses, but he knew that revealing his plan would place his friend's life in danger.

Luther hurried to his hideaway about an hour away. His destination was a stand of thickets located next to the bay. To enter his lair, he crawled on his stomach through a tangle of briars. Close to the water and hidden from view, it was the perfect site for such a secret project. In the center of the clearing, three oak logs sat side by side. Wasting no time, Luther pulled an adz from his bag and went to work. The two end logs had already been tapered and were ready for assembly. Now he worked feverishly on the larger center log, carving out a shallow pit in the middle. Wood chips flew like snowflakes. The sweet fragrances of oak and pine lingered in the air. Luther forced himself to the point of exhaustion. Huffing and puffing, he labored without a break. Time was of the essence if he was to be successful. He knew the weather could change with the next gust of wind.

After he finished, he dragged the three logs to the beach and lashed them together with pieces of rope. "Doesn't have to be to seaworthy, just worthy to see," he mumbled. Finally, the last knot was tied. His ship was ready to be launched.

With a mighty push, the raft skidded across the wet sand and floated in the shallows. Luther climbed aboard. Using a long pole, he pushed the raft into deeper water. When the shoreline disappeared from view, he carefully slipped down into the cockpit of the center log. With an Indian arrowhead, he cut the rigging lines to the other logs and pushed himself free. As the raft drifted back to shore, he began paddling for the other side of the bay. Freedom was just over the horizon. This time he would follow Patayac's advice and head north, crossing the bay instead of the ocean.

The long pole with a shovel blade fastened at each end made a crude but effective paddle. Something from the plantation was finally being put to good use. Luther laughed at the thought of Hunt mocking the slaves. "Keep moving those shovels if you want to be free. You'll either dig a grave or dig your way to China," Hunt would always say. If Hunt could only see those shovels now.

The dugout canoe glided gracefully across the ripples on the bay. The water cooled and refreshed as it splashed against Luther's face. Luther smacked his lips. There was a sweetness to it, like the sweet taste of freedom. By morning, the taste would be even sweeter when he reached land. He only wished Moses could share this moment with him.

"I'm free again," he shouted joyously. This time there was no stopping or turning back. Patayac would be proud. Luther had followed his blueprint for freedom to the smallest detail. He was well on his way to living his dream.

As the first rays of light streaked across the sky, a stiff breeze kicked up the surface of the bay. Whitecaps topped the waves. Minutes later, a hard rain pelted the canoe. Luther fretted. Sweat poured from his face as he lowered his head and plowed through the choppy sea with short, powerful strokes. "Hold the course.

It's not too much farther," he said to himself. With any luck, he hoped to reach the western shore by sunrise. He was afraid his luck was running out in the middle of the bay. As the waves rocked the canoe, the thought occurred to him that he may never see land again.

Unknown to Luther, the bay was being whipped into a froth by a summer squall. With each stroke, he moved deeper into the tempest. The canoe rode the giant swells like a rollercoaster. Higher and higher, then lower and lower. At the bottom of each trough, Luther was smothered by a wall of green, foamy water. "Don't panic! Don't panic!" he shouted. His arms ached as he tried in vain to quicken his pace. Suddenly, a mountainous wave lifted the canoe to the heavens and angrily slammed it down into a swirling whirlpool. "Patayac! Save me!" Luther wailed. The canoe keeled over and disappeared under the roiling sea. Luther had faced the devil in the form of Mr. Hunt hundreds of times. This time he was betwixt another devil and the deep blue sea. The demon swallowed him in one gulp.

Moses stared at the empty blanket and felt guilty. It was the early morning and he was just rolling out of bed. Luther was already hard at work in the fields. Moving to the window, he hoped to spot Luther. Near the manor house, work crews busily cleaned up after last night's storm. Broken limbs littered the lawn. No doubt, Hunt was using Luther's strong back. Moses was sure Luther was in the area. Sooner or later, he would pass by the stable.

"Luther! Luther!" came the cry. Recognizing the urgency in Master Steele's voice, Moses scampered from the loft.

"Where's Luther?" he asked angrily, the veins in his neck bulging.

"In the fields, master. Today was his first day," Moses replied nervously, unaware of Luther's disappearance.

"Well, your friend has disappeared again. I want to know where's my nigger!" Steele screamed as his face turned purple with rage.

"He was here last night sleeping in the loft. That's the last time I saw him," Moses stammered.

"If I find out you know where he is, I'll take every inch of

skin off your back. You'll never live long enough to work the fields."
Steele threw his whip. The braided leather danced at Moses' feet
like a snake ready to strike.

Moses jumped back. He didn't know if he was more afraid of
the whip or Steele. He was shocked at Steele's language. On occasion, he heard Hunt use the word in chastising slaves, but he
never heard it in such a vile and venomous manner. The word
"nigger" cut through his skin like a razor. It was more than a
word. It was life on the plantation. It was white and black and
master and slave. It was a title which separated men from animals.

Moses was humiliated. His whole body burned with a sting-
ing pain. As he looked at Steele, anger filled his eyes. He would
show Steele how proud and defiant a slave could be. Even if he
knew the whereabouts of Luther, he would never tell. The whip
could never hurt as much that word. For the first time, he felt the
agony that belonged to the others. If the master owned the slaves,
then the slaves owned misery. It was their constant companion,
their only possession. It was their only weapon to defeat their foe.

"The dogs are ready," Hunt shouted over the loud barking.
He pulled back hard on the leash to stop the four bloodhounds
from entering the stable.

"Saddle our horses," Steele ordered.

Moses ran to the tack room and returned with the saddles.
As he fumbled nervously with the straps and buckles, Steele
climbed the loft and returned with Luther's blanket. He mounted
his steed and threw the blanket at the baying hounds. In a feeding
frenzy, they ripped it to shreds to pick up Luther's scent.

"Tally-ho! The chase is on," Steele yelled with an evil laugh.
Hunt released the dogs and followed after Steele. Moses watched
them disappear across the fields. He was stunned by the morning's
news. How could his best friend leave without saying good-bye.
He would never see him alive. If Luther was captured, he would
be shot on the spot. Moses pictured Luther running with a heavy
limp a few steps ahead of the bloodhounds as they sniped at his
heels. It was not a pretty sight. Luther was in trouble, and no one
could help. Moses sighed. His first day as stable boy was a disaster, and it was only morning. He would gladly trade it all to go

back in the manor house with his mother.

Late in the afternoon, the search party returned. There was no body being dragged behind the horses. Either they couldn't find Luther or they simply left him where he fell. Steele and Hunt were splattered from head to toe with a layer of light brown mud. Moses grabbed the bridles and led the horses to their stalls. From the scowl on Steele's face, he knew the news was bad. Steele stomped to the manor house, slapping at his thigh with his riding crop and mumbling under his breath. He slammed the door and disappeared for the day.

Later Joseph stopped by the stable. He found Moses staring out the window, hoping for a miracle. Any minute, Moses expected to see Luther walking across the pasture.

"I'm afraid I have bad news for you," Joseph said somberly. "They found a raft washed ashore. On the beach, they found Luther's shirt and shoes."

Moses continued staring out the window, pretending he was deaf. Those dreadful words never reached his ears. Joseph walked over and put his hands on his son's shoulders. "You won't find him out there," he said.

"Maybe, just maybe, he made it back to the shore," Moses whispered as he fought back his tears.

"He's gone forever. The greatest sailor in the world couldn't have made it through last night's storm. It was one of the worst I've ever seen. Perhaps, it's all for the best. Being a runaway for the second time, Master Steele would have worked him to death. At least, he died a free man, not a slave. That's what he always wanted, wasn't it?"

"But they're all gone," Moses sighed. "First Patayac. Now Luther."

"Patayac?" asked a bewildered Joseph. "Who in the world is Patayac?"

Knowing there was no reason to keep Luther's secret, Moses told the story about the Indian holy man. Joseph listened in amazement. He heard Indian stories from the older slaves, but he never laid eyes on a real one. At the docks, he saw mulattoes who worked as deck hands, but they were more white than red.

"He said my future is my past. To know myself, I must know

my ancestors, my father and my father's father."

"Sounds like he was a very wise man," Joseph mused as his voice faded into silence. "But who am I? I know you are my father, but I know little else. Should I know about my ancestors?" Moses asked eagerly.

Joseph was startled by the questions. He paused for a moment to collect his thoughts.

"Patayac was right," he replied. "But your future is in your distant past. I was born a slave and will die a slave. But your grandfather was born a free man, even though he died a slave. That is where we will begin."

"Then you will teach me?" Moses asked.

Joseph rubbed his chin and raised a furrowed brow. "Of course. You are no longer a child. You must learn about the world, but it is not something you can learn in one day. Remember Luther and Patayac. Think about them and what I have told you. Every man, good or bad, is a teacher. Learn the lessons they teach."

With those words, a smile came to Moses' face. For the first time in his life, he saw a different side to the man who was the most humble and obedient of slaves. He saw more than a man who worked from sunrise to sundown without a whimper; he saw a man who knew how to survive. "Oh yes, master! Your good old boy Joseph will do that for you," he often heard his father say. Many slaves mocked his father, calling him a bootlick, an "Uncle Tom" or worse. But the joke was on them. His father was a crafty actor, smarter and more cunning than Master Steele. His father did what he had to do for his family, whether he liked it or not.

On the way back to the cabin, Joseph questioned his promise to Moses. Native customs were strictly forbidden. A slave could lose his tongue for speaking a word of his native language. Was it worth the risk, he asked himself over and over. The question rekindled memories of his childhood days on the plantation. Joseph remembered his own father, but the memories were vague. There wasn't a chance to learn about the man. His father died when he was a young boy. It was something he always regretted. He wished he could have his father back for just a few hours.

After weighing all the options, Joseph decided it was worth the risk. There were things in life that needed to be learned at any cost. Most likely, this was a once in a lifetime opportunity to teach his son. Joseph reluctantly had to admit it. His son was growing up. Moses was no longer a boy but a young man. Tomorrow he could be sold downriver. The knowledge of his family would be his life preserver.

Slave owners made their fortunes by uprooting people from their native lands and replanting them in foreign soil. Slaves produced fruit for a short time, then withered on the vine and died. Patayac was right. The history of the Indians was no different than the Africans. His words were a warning to all nations. We must plant the seed of life by teaching one another. If we do, then one day the roots of these tribes will take hold in the soil. From one mighty tree, a mighty forest will grow.

Chapter Four—

Of Drums and Drummers

School was held every Sunday, the only day of the week the slaves were off. In the afternoons, Joseph and Moses walked far into the woods, away from the sights and sounds of the plantation. In a secluded spot, they learned about life and each other. For most of the lessons, Joseph talked and Moses questioned.

"Your grandfather's name was Patunde Opatunji. He was a master drummer with the Yorubu tribe on the west coast of Africa along the Niger River. One day he was captured and sold into slavery. His sacred drum was tossed into the ocean and lost forever. Never again would he drum. He died after coming to America. His body was placed in the ground without ceremony. The gods were insulted and punished him. He was not allowed to join his ancestors in the spirit world. Today, his spirit walks the earth searching for Olodumare, the Supreme Being, owner of the heaven. He calls out to Olodumare to free him and his people, but Olodumare cannot hear him because of Shango. Shango, the god of thunder, travels the skies and muffles the voices of those souls imprisoned on earth. A master drummer needs his drum to speak with gods. Opatunji needs to find his drum. Until that time, no one will be free."

"Can I free Opatunji?" Moses asked hopefully.

"That I cannot answer, but I do know that somewhere in the universe there is someone who can."

Although Joseph was born a slave, he had a vast knowledge of African people and customs. In the evening, he often talked with the older slaves and listened to their stories. Like Patayac, he stored the information in his head and hoped one day to collect the history of his people. Since his father had been a master drummer, he tried to learn as much as he could about drums and drummers. But slaves with this kind of experience were far and few in between. When Joseph met one, he picked his brain clean.

While his knowledge was limited, it was enough to whet the appetite of his student. Moses learned about the dundun, a hourglass tension drum used as the primary instrument by the master drummer. This "talking drum," was the voice of the people and used to tell stories and announce the news. But the drum had a revered place in tribal society. Above all else, it was the only instrument to call upon the gods. In the anointed hands of the master drummer, the drum beckoned the gods to hear the prayers of the village. By pressing the thongs which connected the drumheads and squeezing the drum with his free hand, the drummer mimicked the Yoruba language.

"The master drummer is a symbol of his people. His spirit must be one with the gods," Joseph preached. "When the earth was created, a giant drum was struck. The vibrations from the drum struck the earth and brought it to life. Every living thing was given a special rhythm. When the master drummer is able to hear and feel all of these rhythms, he will have the power to talk to the gods through his drum."

Moses was an outstanding student. He quickly learned to identify all of the sounds in the forest. His ears became acutely tuned to nature. He easily distinguished between the sounds of the sparrow and the blue jay, whether it sang or flapped its wings. He knew the difference in the wind, whether it whistled through the pine tree or oak, and whether it carried rain or snow. Every sound produced a unique rhythm which vibrated through his body.

Even during the day, Moses learned his lessons. The stable was a classroom which overwhelmed the senses. Every animal had its own unique sounds, whether eating, sleeping or breathing. Each horse had a distinctive click when it walked or galloped. He knew when they were hungry or tired by the tone of their snorting. It was no accident that Hunt always found him hard at work. The agitated overseer always walked away in disgust, disappointed that he was unable to administer a tongue lashing. Little did he know that Moses could hear the click of his boot heels a hundred yards away.

Moses heard the rhythms and felt the vibrations. He was ready to graduate to a higher level of study. His goal was to become a master drummer. But before he could become one with the drum, he had to become a drummer. Joseph could teach him why he had to become a drummer but not how. If he was to succeed, he had to teach himself. Again, he looked to the natural world as his teacher. Nature asked only that you open your eyes, ears and heart to learn. Everyday, rain or shine, Moses practiced his lessons.

The air was filled with the music of the universe, and every sound had its own cadence. Moses easily reproduced the most intricate beats, whether it was his father's hammer or a woodpecker hammering. Using finger, thumb and palm strokes, he layered patterns to build a symphony of percussion. Wood buckets in the stable were ideal drums.

A summer storm was his favorite conductor, and rain, his favorite musician. The beating, splashing and dripping water offered the stiffest challenge to his skills. Rain forever improvised on its rhythms. The water was alive as it bounced off objects inside and outside the stable. The sounds were mysterious and seductive. The patterns were intricate and imaginative. Single, double and triple strokes echoed about the stable. Moses cataloged each one of these rhythms to create his own musical library.

The lessons had gone well. So well that in late fall, Joseph decided Moses was ready for his first field trip. Late one evening, he roused Moses from his bed.

"Moses! Get up. We're going to the Graves," he whispered.

"The Graves plantation?" Moses replied in bewilderment.

Surely, he must be dreaming. No slave in his right mind would go there. The Graves family was the largest planter in the region, employing over a hundred slaves in the tobacco fields. Master Graves was a stern disciplinarian who readily administered the whip for the slightest infraction. "From cradle to Graves" was the standing joke among his slaves. The place was hell on earth. Compared to the Graves place, the Steele plantation was a paradise. No slave dared to set foot on the property without a pass. To be caught trespassing was a death sentence.

"Near the plantation, not on it," said Joseph, sensing Moses' hesitation. "We're certainly not going to knock on that devil's door and dine at his table."

They headed east, circled around town, and followed the main road. At a sharp curve, they turned off into the woods. Following a trail of natural landmarks, they walked for about two miles until they spotted a large campfire. Creeping to within fifty yards of a clearing, they watched. Around the fire, a group of black men, wearing loincloths, spoke in strange tongues. Their faces and chests were streaked with white paint in geometric patterns. Strips of animal fur adorned their arms and legs. Some carried crude spears, nothing more than long, pointed sticks, and shields of animal skin. They reminded Moses of how Patayac looked on the night he died.

"They come to celebrate the traditional harvest and remember their native customs," Joseph explained. "For one night of the year, they are free again. They meet as tribal warriors not as slaves. They risk their lives to carry on their heritage. They are brave men."

Dancers formed two circles in opposite directions around the fire. They walked slowly with hesitating steps. On signal from the leader, they froze in position and chanted. Outside the circle, in the shadows of the trees, musicians played a variety of homemade drums and flutes.

As the tempo of the music increased, Moses closed his eyes and listened. He heard the intricate rhythms and pictured the hands of the drummers racing across the drumskins. He dissected each rhythm and committed it to memory. The cadences were more sophisticated than the rain. One beat after another was layered on top of a central rhythm. When the drumming reached a crescendo, the dancers raced to the beat. When the drumming stopped, they toppled over in exhaustion, literally swept off of their feet by the music. When the drumming started up, the dancers were back on their feet without missing a beat. Moses knew the drummers had breathed life into the dancers. These men may not have been master drummers but they knew how to awaken the spirit of the drum.

"Patrollers," Joseph warned. "Get down!"

Moses heard the snapping of tree branches and fell to his stomach. Galloping horses passed next to him, almost on top of him. Seconds later, the drumming was drowned out by the thunder of hooves. Moses lifted his head and watched in horror as the riders charged the circle from different directions. Two groups of about ten men, wearing masks and carrying long-handled clubs, swarmed over the dancers. As the dancers attempted to flee, they were struck on the head and shoulders. Painful screams filled the air as blows rained down with a dull thud or sharp crack. Flesh was bruised and bones were broken.

When the last bloodied dancer crawled into the woods, the riders gathered around the dying fire. They sipped whiskey from a brown jug and laughed at their folly. Moses watched in disgust as the men started to parade around the fire and mimic the dancers. They stopped intermittently and tilted their heads. Howling at the moon, they echoed a foul stream of blasphemy. For the grand finale to their mockery, they gathered the spears and shields and threw them into the fire with one final curse. As they departed, Moses noticed an unusual blaze on one of the horses. The long, white streak, shaped like an hourglass, seemed to glow in the dark. It was an unforgettable birthmark forever etched in his mind.

"What will happen to the dancers?" Moses asked.

"Next year they will find a new place to celebrate, and once again, the patrollers will track them down. To them, it is a hunt, a sick sport like chasing a wounded fox."

"Did you ever celebrate the harvest with the dancers?" Moses asked.

"I was either too scared or too smart to join them. To be honest, these are not my customs. I was born in America, not Africa. My link with my native land has been broken. But remember in the depths of our souls, the same fire burns within us. Our passing thoughts move across the light from that fire and cast shadows. These shadows are the same for every man who is bonded by slavery. In our hearts, we all are shadow drummers, beating the drum for freedom."

"I understand," Moses replied, somewhat embarrassed that he had put his father on the spot with such a personal question, and somewhat mystified by his father's winding answer. Of course, he knew what his father was talking about. Since the deaths of Patayac and Luther, his own spirit had been smothered by dark clouds of despair. After some soul searching, he finally glimpsed the spirit of hope that dwelled in the depths of every slave. However, more mystifying was his father's talk about freedom. It was the first time he had heard him mention the word. More and more, his father was sounding like Luther. Moses couldn't decide if that was good or bad.

The stable was quiet when Moses returned. The horses were bedded down comfortably on the cool autumn night. From his vantage point in the loft, he noticed the horse in the far corner pacing nervously in his stall. Just a strange coincidence, he thought as he climbed back down to check on his hunch. He reached over the rail and lifted the heavy blanket. Steam rose from the horse's back. The hide was hot and wet. When the horse jerked its head to the side, the white blaze hit Moses squarely in the eyes. His guess about the hourglass was correct. Mister Hunt was a night rider.

He checked other horses. None of them had been ridden. At least he knew that Master Steele was not a vigilante. Back in the loft, he wondered how much time was left in Hunt's hourglass. He knew the last grains of sand were rapidly spilling to the bottom. Time had run out for Luther. Now time was running out for him.

On a Sunday afternoon in late November, Joseph and Moses took their last walk. The day was cloudy and gray without a whisper of wind. The bitter cold of an early winter stripped away the last of the summer's disguises. The dazzling greens had faded into sickly shades of brown. The plantation was naked and cold like a rotting corpse.

Joseph returned to the place where he gave the first lesson. As he and Moses took their customary positions, snow flakes began to fall. Within a few minutes, the frozen ground was covered with a fine dusting. The perfect day for the final examination, Joseph thought. Just as the plantation was revealing its true ugliness, the heavens dressed it in a beautiful cloak of white. Moses sat silently and waited for the lesson to begin.

"You have journeyed a thousand miles over the past months, yet you haven't left the plantation. You have made a thousand friends, yet you haven't met a single stranger. What you have done is traveled to the inner sanctum of your soul to discover your true self. Now you must be prepared to travel outside yourself in the world. Before you know where you must go, you must know where you have been. There is only one question that will lead you to the road of salvation."

"I'm ready," Moses replied calmly.

"What do you hear, Moses?" Joseph asked solemnly.

"Only the silence of winter."

"Close your eyes and listen," Joseph instructed. After a few minutes of silence, Joseph again questioned his student. "What do you hear?"

"I hear my heart beat. I feel a pulsating rhythm which vibrates through by body. I feel my spirit as one with the universe."

Moses had passed the exam. A quick smile came to Joseph's face. His student had excelled beyond his hopes. There were no more lessons to be learned in the classroom. "I have taught you all that I know. You are a remarkable student," Joseph said with delight. "You have learned the secrets of the soul. You have found the spirit of the drummer. Now you must find the spirit of the drum. It is a journey which can take one day or a hundred years."

"One day, will I be able to free the spirit of Opatunji?" Moses asked.

"Remember all that you have learned. Never stop learning and never give up hope. One day, you may find the wisdom to solve that mystery."

Walking back to the plantation, Joseph was astounded by the insight of his son. In a year, he had grown from a humble houseboy to a confident young man. There was something special, yet mysterious, about this child. He saw a purpose that was beyond his reasoning. As they approached the cabin, he patted his son on the back. "Walk tall from this day forward. Your grandfather is proud that you are following in his footsteps."

Chapter Five—

A Very Merry Christmas

The beginning of December marked the start of the Christmas season. Despite the cold weather, a lukewarm relationship developed between master and slave. Although this uneasy truce would end in a few weeks, everyone put a smile on their face and tried to enjoy the holiday. For the slaves, it was their only chance during the year to have some fun. Women spent their days in the kitchen cooking for the Christmas Day feast. Children swept every nook and cranny in the manor house. Many of the men worked on wood crafts. In the light of a fireplace, calloused hands whittled ornaments from blocks of softwood. The wildlife figures, such as ducks and deer, were so realistic that Master Steele gave them as gifts to his influential friends. Even the nativity scene, which was the mantle centerpiece in the manor house, was carved by a long-forgotten slave.

No one was busier than Moses. He worked non-stop from dawn to dusk. Everyday there were more shopping trips and social visits. To meet the hectic schedule, horses and carriages had to be ready at a moment's notice. If Christmas was the busiest season, then Christmas Eve was the busiest day of the year for the stable boy. Moses spent the evening armed with a jar of polish and a handful of rags. Every bit, bridle, and saddle was cleaned and polished. Even the family coach was hand-buffed to a mirror finish.

On Christmas morning, Moses was up before the sun. By the feeble light of a small lantern, he groomed the Cleveland Bays for their trip into town. As he worked, he remembered the Bible story about the birth of baby Jesus. His mother recited it every Christmas to the slave children. Images of shepherds in a field and wise men bearing gifts danced in his head. What gift would he, a lowly stable boy, have brought, he wondered. Closing his eyes, he leaned back and imagined what it must have been like hundreds of years ago on that first Christmas day. As he slowly opened them, he almost expected to find himself sitting at the feet of the newborn king. There was no better place to be on Christmas Eve than in a stable.

The coach team enjoyed being pampered. Moses brushed the coats of these hulking, brown horses to a silky sheen. After oiling their hooves, he braided the black manes and tails as a final touch. Stepping back to admire his handiwork, the horses snorted, then nodded their heads in approval.

"Merry Christmas, Moses," greeted Joseph as he entered the stable. The smile which streaked his face was as bright and shiny as the brass buttons on his jacket. In his coachman's uniform, he looked like a military officer. All he needed was a sword at his side. Moses chuckled at the sight. He easily pictured his father standing between General Washington and Colonel Steele.

"And don't forget these," Joseph said, handing two sets of sleigh bells to Moses. "All we need now is some snow, and we'll have a Christmas like you see in those fancy picture books."

Joseph drove the Steele family to St. Michael's for church services. In the meantime, house servants readied the ballroom for the holiday feast. Chairs were collected from every room so that each guest had a comfortable seat. Long planks were brought in from the barn and covered with the finest linens to make a gigantic banquet table.

At eleven o'clock, the jingle of sleigh bells in the lane signaled the start of dinner. Slaves dressed in their Sunday clothes walked briskly to the rear of the kitchen. As the guests lined up, Moses waited impatiently in the stable for his father. He had a good reason to be excited. This was his first Christmas in the ballroom, instead of his customary place in the kitchen with the children. As the stable boy, he had finally earned his place at the banquet table. He didn't want to chance losing his seat.

"We're late, Papa. Hurry, before they run out of food."

"The impatience of youth. They wouldn't think of eating until the coachman arrives. Christmas tradition! They know the slower I drive, the hungrier they get," replied Joseph with a hearty laugh.

The cavernous ballroom was aglow from the light of a hundred bayberry candles which filled the air with a fragrant warmth. Holly wreaths trimmed with red ribbons hung in the windows. In the far corner stood the family Christmas tree. The large white pine tree, nearly fifteen feet high, was decorated with cookies and ornaments from top to bottom.

Once everyone was seated, Master Steele rose from his chair at the head of the table and offered a toast. Glasses of brandy were lifted in the air. Moses downed the contents of his glass without a second thought. Yuk! What a foul concoction," he said to himself. "How can anyone drink this stuff?"

The brandy burned his throat and watered his eyes. If only his tears could reach his stomach, he might feel better. He laughed quietly at the thought. Lowering his glass, he looked at the faces around the table. They were all the same, eyes, ears, noses, lips and teeth. Drinking the finest brandy money could buy were farmers, carpenters, cooks, and seamstresses. Not a slave in sight, just ordinary people whose skin happened to be brown.

When Master Steele was seated, servants brought out trays piled high with ham, venison, turkey, sweet potatoes, green beans and corn biscuits. When the last crumbs of the apple pie were devoured and the table cleared, the celebration moved to the barn. The real Christmas festivities were ready to begin.

The building was already crowded with slaves from nearby plantations lucky enough to secure a pass. Master Steele was a stern master, but at Christmas he had the reputation of putting on the best frolic for miles around. Within minutes, the sounds of fiddles and banjos filled the air. Couples immediately spilled onto the dance floor. The old women and young children formed a circle and clapped for their favorite dancers. Outside, the men stuffed their pipes with the best of last year's tobacco crop and gossiped about their masters. Just inside the main door, a long line formed at the large oak barrel, filled to the brim with the finest of plantation whiskey.

Moses spent most the evening watching the revelry from a distance. This year's celebration was not the same without Luther.

Looking across the dance floor, he pictured Luther kicking up his heels. Even with his bad foot, he could spin the young ladies with the best of any dancers. No doubt, he would have hounded Moses into taking to the dance floor with one of the girls. Too shy to dance, Moses was always content being a wallflower with the other boys his age. But if dancing would bring Luther back, he was ready to dance until dawn.

Joseph found Moses standing next to the musicians. "Let's take a walk," he said. "I'm afraid I'm getting too old for all of this excitement."

They walked in the direction of the blacksmith shop. In the background, the music from the barn languished in the night. Inside the small shop, warm air still rose from the hearth. Moses rubbed his hands over the glowing embers as his father lit a lantern. He could only wonder about what his father was doing in the shop on Christmas night.

"Close your eyes and hold out your hands," Joseph instructed as he reached beneath his workbench. A second later, Moses felt a bulky object drop into his palms. "My Christmas gift to you."

Moses opened his eyes. It was a drum, a real honest-to-goodness drum. He gently cradled it like a newborn baby, caressing the smooth shell with his fingers. The drum was a small wooden nail keg approximately eighteen inches in length and twelve inches in diameter. The lids were replaced by goatskins which were pinched into place by barrel hoops. Simple yet sophisticated, primitive yet professional, it was the work of a master craftsman. No detail was left unattended. The shell had been stained brown, the drumheads bleached white, and the barrel hoops painted black.

"It's the most beautiful drum I have ever seen," Moses said graciously. "But I feel bad because I have no gift for you."

"One day you will do the same for your son. The true gift is giving, not receiving. That is what Christmas is all about."

Placing the drum in his lap, Moses tapped lightly on the head. It had a deep, mellow sound which rattled the metal clutter hanging from the beams. Raising his right hand high in the air, he struck a sharp blow. Like a bolt of lightning, the drum vibrated in every part of his body. A tingling sensation spread from his head to his toes.

"This drum is our secret. Play it only when you are alone," Joseph warned. "Now let's get back to the frolic. I'm sure the pretty girls are waiting for you."

Instead of returning to the barn, Moses raced to the loft. Tonight he needed time to be alone. He sat by the window where Luther often sat and gazed at the dark blue sky. He played his drum softly, mirroring the rhythms of the twinkling stars. Moses was excited about Christmas, but most of his thoughts were on Luther. Somewhere in the vast universe, there must be a lucky star for everyone, he mused. If he had only one wish in the world, it would be to bring back his friend. His fingers slowed to a stop as he remembered the words of his father. "He's gone forever," echoed over and over in his mind. Moses clenched his teeth and swallowed hard to fight back the tears. His eyes searched the heavens to wish upon the brightest star.

The first day of 1813 marked the end of the holiday season. Moses hoped the new year would be better for him and his family, but things were not off to a promising start. Any remnants of "goodwill toward men" evaporated with the return of Mister William Hunt, overseer of the Steele empire. To Hunt, Christmas never existed. It never existed because he refused to socialize with the slaves. With the permission of Master Steele, he excused himself from the holiday. It was rumored that he was once an indentured servant to the Steele family at another plantation. Toiling next to the slaves, he slowly bought his freedom, day by day, penny by penny. He was so humiliated by the ordeal, he vowed revenge on every master and slave.

Hunt never smiled, not even in the company of his own family. A wicked sneer creased his face like a grotesque scar. A sneer and a whip, those were his trademarks. He needed no other introductions.

While Master Steele was a cold-hearted businessman, Hunt was a cold-hearted dictator who took a perverse delight in making life a living hell. Now that Luther was gone, Moses was certain he would be the object of his contempt. Being the total opposite of Luther in personality didn't matter. What mattered was color. In Hunt's mind, color separated right from wrong, smart from stupid, and most importantly, him from the slaves. Color was his reason to hate, and he wore his hatred on his sleeve for everyone to see.

Hunt's insecurity was his motivation. Neither master nor slave, he knew the status of his position and its value. The plantation could run without him, but not without the others. Everyday he had to prove his worth, regardless of who or what got in his way. He was especially jealous of anyone who curried the favor of his boss. Compliments by Master Steele about his new stable boy merely fanned a smoldering fire. Hunt cringed every time a kind word was spoken. Moses had to be on constant alert. Hunt was lurking in the shadows. A showdown was inevitable. Moses didn't know how sudden it would be, but the hourglass was running dry.

"Saddle up the master's horse," Hunt yelled into the stable.

Moses immediately dropped his rake and ran to the tack room. Returning with the saddle, he stopped dead in his tracks. He watched in horror as Hunt threw his whip against the back of Cyclone, Master Steele's riding horse. The stallion reared up in pain with fire in his eyes.

"We'll see how Master Steele likes it after he finds out you whipped his prized possession," Hunt shouted angrily. He cocked his arm a second time. Whissh! The whip sliced through the air with an evil hiss. Moses rushed to the front of Cyclone and raised his hand to his face. He grimaced in pain as the whip coiled around his forearm like a snake, biting and squeezing his flesh. He flung his arm backwards. The whip fell harmlessly from Hunt's hand.

Hunt's face turned blood red. "You dare strike your master," he screamed at the top of his lungs. "I'll teach you a lesson about master and slave that you'll carry on your back for the rest of your life."

Moses had to think quickly. His only hope was to outsmart Hunt and beat him at his own game. He knew Steele would never believe the word of a slave. He had to fight fire with fire. As Hunt bent down to grab the whip, Moses jerked his arm back again. Hunt scrambled on the ground as the whip skittered from his reach. A few more jerks on the whip brought Hunt to within inches of Moses' feet. Hunt slowly rose. Once face to face with him, Hunt raised his fist high over his head to strike a killing blow.

"I know who you are," Moses said in a bold but quivering voice. "You're a night rider. If Master Steele finds out, you'll be tarred and feathered. No more fine cabin, fine clothes, or fine niggers to whip."

The verbal counterpunch was a knockout blow. Hunt stopped dead in his tracks. He was stunned that someone knew his secret. The boy was right. If Steele found out he was damaging property, he would be banished from the plantation. His face turned a sickly, pale white. He clenched his teeth then spit a stream of tobacco juice on the ground.

"Why I think we just struck a deal between us," Hunt said sarcastically as he picked up the whip. "But remember this, boy. Don't ever get in my way or you'll end up like your friend, Luther."

After Hunt walked away, Moses breathed a sigh of relief. He had come face to face with the devil and lived to tell about it. He rubbed the welt on his forearm and reached down to cup his trembling knees. Hunt had declared war. Moses won the first battle, but it was only a matter of time before Hunt would attack again.

Chapter Six—

The British Are Coming

With the arrival of spring, Colonel Steele, patriarch of the Steele family and Revolutionary War hero, became a frequent visitor to the stable. In the winter months, he occasionally stopped by the stable to chat and tell war stories. But now he came with a purpose. When the local militia sought help in defending the town, the colonel eagerly volunteered his expertise. Although close to seventy years old, the former aide-de-camp to General Washington at Valley Forge still rode and shot like a second lieutenant.

When the British fleet was sighted on the Chesapeake, Steele boldly predicted St. Michael's would be attacked by the end of the summer. The shipyards were the target, he professed. The British had to stop the construction of privateers—sleek, fast sailing vessels which harassed the fleet.

Dressed smartly in a military uniform, the colonel rode into town at least twice a week, often spending the night. The war and the warm weather breathed new life into the aging warrior.

"Saddle up two horses. Today you're going with me," the colonel announced.

"But what will Master Steele say?" Moses protested mildly.

"Sometimes I think people forget who really owns this plantation," the colonel joked. "Until they lay me to rest, I'll give the orders around here. And besides, you're the only one who listens to my stories. It's time you see how I make them up."

The trips to town were leisurely. The colonel filled the time with talk about the war. At times, the colonel spoke like a grizzled veteran to a young recruit. Moses enjoyed that. He liked being part of the colonel's private army. It was as close to any army as he was going to get. The colonel's house may have been built in a tobacco field, but his home was firmly rooted in the bloodied soil of a battlefield.

Crack! Boom! Crack! Boom! Musket and cannon fire ripped through the air as infantry and artillery units practiced. A cloud of white smoke, peppered with burnt gunpowder, blanketed the field. On any given day, hundreds of uniformed militia, known as St. Michael's Patriotic Blues, drilled. Moses always stood off to the side where the drummers, usually four strong, sounded the commands. To the beat of the drum, soldiers moved forward and backwards like puppets on a string.

Moses was amazed at the enthusiasm of these citizen soldiers, but puzzled by their attitude. They freely gave their time, and most likely, would grudgingly give their lives. Freedom was the cause. "Liberty or death" was the battle cry. They were willing to fight for their freedom, but weren't willing to free others. They could free the slaves without spilling a single drop of blood. To Moses, it was a totally illogical situation.

As the unofficial aide to the colonel, Moses made the trip to St. Michael's at least once a week. By June, every able man, to include Master Steele and Mister Hunt, had been trained for military duty. Most could march and shoot as well as the regulars. The only question was how well would they fight. The colonel felt confident that with the right strategy the militia could repel any British invasion.

At the end of July, British ships were spotted at the mouth of the river. The war was rapidly heating up. The colonel's prediction was coming true. To monitor the situation, the colonel took up residence at the old church which served as the military headquarters. In August, a British frigate was seen on the river taking soundings. The town was put on alert. The attack was only days away.

In the late afternoon of August 9th, the colonel unexpectedly returned to the plantation. "Just cool her down," he said as he handed Moses the reins. "Looks like the British will be attacking tonight or tomorrow. I'll be heading back with Master Steele and Mister Hunt. Saddle their horses."

The colonel returned with Steele and Hunt in tow. With

swords clanging at their sides, they trudged reluctantly behind their commander. There was no doubt the colonel was itching for a good fight. Likewise, there was no doubt that if the fate of the town rested in the hands of Master Steele and Mister Hunt, it would slip through their sweaty palms. They moved as if their boots were mired in mud and mounted their horses as if the saddles were greased.

"Come on boys!" the colonel exhorted. "There's a war on. The British are coming back for another whipping."

After the trio departed, Moses sprinted to the blacksmith shop. "Papa! Papa!" he yelled. "The British are attacking tonight. What should we do?"

Joseph calmed his son and listened to the latest news. "We will do absolutely nothing," he said to Moses' surprise. "There is nothing to get excited about. This is not our battle. This is English fighting English. They are still fighting a war they started decades ago. Now go back to the stable and don't say a word to anyone. I don't want everyone getting riled. We're already a conquered people; doesn't make much difference if we're conquered again. They can't make us slaves. We're already that. Our day to do battle will come. Today is not the day."

Moses couldn't believe his ears. He shrugged his shoulders and dejectedly walked back to the stable. One day his father speaks about freedom; the next day he doesn't want to even talk about it. The man was hard to figure. He was certain his father would have rallied the slaves to defend the plantation.

Back in the loft, Moses studied the situation. "I must act," he declared brashly. "I am the grandson of Opatunji, a great African warrior." He remembered the colonel's briefing to militia leaders. The colonel was convinced the British would bombard the town from the sea and sweep in from the western flank. Militia leaders thought otherwise. They believed the British fleet would sail straight into the harbor. To Moses, the number of ships at the mouth of the river only confirmed the colonel's belief.

"I know the place where they will land," he announced confidently. "I can stop them."

Late that evening, Moses retrieved his drum and headed for a remote section of the river where he walked the shoreline towards town. Locating the village lights, he marked a spot in the sand with a stick. He planned to patrol the beach for a couple hundred yards in each direction. When the British arrived, he would sound the alarm.

The night was perfect for an attack. Rain clouds covered the moon and shrouded the river in total darkness. A light drizzle masked the river. After hours of listening to waves lap the beach, Moses decided to rethink his strategy. Quite possibly, the colonel may have been wrong. After all, his plan had been voted down by the militia commanders. For the next hour, he sat on the beach, reminding himself of the colonel's plan. He needed a lot of convincing. He was wet, tired and ready to go home.

Moses had dozed off when suddenly his head snapped back and his eyes popped open. He turned an ear toward the river. Something was moving. A fish or a fleet? In the black void, he could only hear it. The sound wasn't really a noise, but rather a break in the rhythm of the waves.

Moses moved to the edge of the water. Is my mind playing tricks or did I actually hear something? he wondered. Again, he listened and again, he heard the sound. He closed his eyes and concentrated. There, he heard it again, only this time more clearly. A curious cadence drifted across the river. Closer and closer came the soft, swish of oars being pulled against the water.

There was no time to waste. Any second the long boats would run aground. Moses darted into the tall grass and rigged a sling for his drum from his rope belt. Placing the drum sideways against his stomach, he slowly and softly sounded the cadences he heard from the regimental drummers. Minute by minute, he gradually increased the volume of his strokes until his hands stung the drumheads. He drummed with a passion and fury. Da-rum! Da-rum! Da-rum-dum-dum! Dum-dum! Drum rolls echoed up and down the beach from a parade of drummers. When the drumming reached a crescendo, he lowered his voice and bellowed commands to his invisible army. "Right flank! Present arms! Prepare to fire!" he barked.

When he could not longer lift his arms, he collapsed to his knees in total exhaustion. He held his breath and listened. Once again, small waves gently lapped the shore. Perhaps, the British turned back or landed farther down the beach, he thought. He crawled onto the beach and listened for a few more minutes. Perhaps, they were drifting on the water as a trick or perhaps, all of this had been a figment of his imagination.

With all of the racket, Moses was certain someone had heard him. Fearing for his life, he picked up his drum and ran like the wind. When he reached the edge of the plantation, he hid the drum under a pile of leaves. Back in the safety of the loft, he replayed the night's events. If what he had heard was a scouting party, in all likelihood, it was only one boat. Most likely, the massive invasion force was still anchored in the river. After some deliberation over the merit of his efforts, he fell asleep. He was satisfied and content. At least he had tried to save the town.

Moses tossed and turned throughout the night. Little did he realize the thunder which awakened him during the early morning was cannonade by the British navy. At four o'clock that morning, eleven barges with nearly three hundred soldiers and marines landed at Parrott's Point, a knob of land at the mouth of the harbor with a small fort. The British successfully stormed the fort, but for some unexplained reason, they returned to their barges. Unable to penetrate the harbor entrance, they retreated to the middle of the river and bombed away. British gunners, fooled by the fog and the lanterns hanging in the treetops, overshot their intended targets. Most of the six-pound balls flew over the town without damage.

Colonel Steele, who weathered the initial attack in the church basement, emerged to direct the counterattack. As he sat high in the saddle, the night exploded directly overhead. One, maybe two shots cut the church steeple in half. The huge brass bell snapped from its mounting and fell to the earth like a meteor. Clung! It sank five feet in the mud. Craassh! The top of the steeple hit the ground like a bomb and exploded into a million pieces.

Things happened so fast, the colonel could only watch in horror. There was no escape. He pulled hard on the reins as his horse reared up and kicked the air. Leaning forward to balance himself, a sharp pain stabbed him in the chest. "I'm hit," he cried out in agony. He gasped for air, sucked in a deep breath, then slumped to the side.

The terrified horse bolted through the streets. At dawn, soldiers found the horse grazing in the town square. The lifeless body of the colonel dangled from the saddle.

Chapter Seven—

A Reward for Bravery

Colonel Bradford Cornelius Steele was buried with full military honors. Regimental drummers led the funeral procession as muffled drums sounded a mournful march. A slow parade of politicians, military officers, merchants, and planters trailed behind the hearse. The colonel was laid to rest beneath the old Wye oak next to his beloved wife. One chapter in the Steele family, a most glamourous and glorious episode, had been completed. The next chapter was ready to unfold.

The slaves were allowed to pay their last respects. They merely lowered their heads and mutely filed past the mahogany casket. Back in the fields, the older ones reminisced about the good times when the colonel was the master. All agreed he was a just man who treated his slaves like family members. Like the slaves, he was a prisoner on his own plantation. He was a fighter not a farmer, a soldier not a slave owner. Both he and slaves knew it. Perhaps, that's why he treated his slaves with dignity. They shared a common bond.

With the colonel gone, many slaves feared that Hunt would wrestle control of the plantation from Master Steele. It wasn't hard to imagine. Master Steele was a man of leisure, a sportsman at heart. He treated the plantation like a hobby. That didn't mean he was an inept businessman. It just meant he was more interested in the finer things in life, and had enough money to pursue those interests.

Moses was concerned. He believed it was just a matter of time before Hunt made his presence known. Up until his death, the colonel was a steady influence. Although his son ran the plantation, he was still the owner. People acted accordingly. Moses was convinced that Hunt avoided the stable because of the colonel. Now there was nothing to stop him from his revenge. And if that wasn't enough of a problem, there was the latest rumor. Town leaders had formed a special war committee to investigate the battle.

The town of St. Michael's quickly returned to its normal routine. The day after the attack, merchants stocked shelves and swept floors, while shipwrights cut planks and caulked seams. The maritime business didn't miss a beat. Ships arrived and departed on schedule. On the Steele plantation, the interruption was negligible. After the colonel's funeral, the slaves went back to the fields. Many of them didn't even know there was a battle. Those who did know were disheartened by the British loss. They felt that being kidnapped by the Royal Navy was better than remaining captured on the plantation. Their false hopes had been buoyed by rumors that kidnapped slaves were being released on their own.

The day after the funeral, Master Steele rode into town to serve on the war committee. His interest was self-serving. He volunteered because of his father's death. How the colonel died without a mark on his body was one of the mysteries to be explored by the committee.

Early that morning, Joseph stopped by the stable. "Master Steele will be ready to leave any minute. His horse better be ready to go," Joseph warned.

"What do you think will happen today?" Moses asked anxiously.

"They'll make some old fool a war hero and add some fancy lies to their history books."

"Do you think they'll ask questions about the attack?"

"Shouldn't be too many. I think everyone is glad the British just gave up and went home."

Moses went back to work. Nothing to worry about, he figured. No one saw him leave the stable on the night of the attack, or else rumors would be in the air.

By the time Master Steele arrived at the town hall, an overflowing crowd was milling outside. This was the biggest event in years. Rumors about conspiracies, traitors and spies flew from everyone's lips.

The meeting was called to order with a rap of the gavel. The colonel's death was the first item on the agenda. There was only one witness. The town doctor testified that the colonel died from a heart attack brought on by the rigors of battle—inquiry closed. The committee voted unanimously to award the colonel a medal for bravery posthumously.

When the Battle of St. Michael's was addressed, the committee publicly announced the British defeat was due to the heroic efforts of the local militia. However, behind closed doors, it was the accepted opinion that the British failure was due to their own bungling of military tactics. This left one question unanswered. Despite hours of testimony from citizens and soldiers, no one could answer why the British stopped the attack after their initial success. The gallery concluded this was one of those mysteries that will never be answered.

Hurrying to wrap things up and return home, the committee moved to the final item. Spectators in the courtroom expected a quick explanation to the strange sounds which came from northwest of the town. Most townspeople claimed it was thunder or a cannon. A few dared to say drums. Everyone had an opinion, but no one had an answer.

The incessant chatter was abruptly silenced by the appearance of a young Negro. Everyone gawked as the barefoot man, dressed only in a pair of ragged trousers, was escorted to the head table.

"Ladies and gentlemen," the chairman of the committee announced. "We shall attempt to determine the cause of the British retreat. I'm sure you will find this next witness most informative and, perhaps, somewhat entertaining."

Spectators were bewildered. Only a few minutes ago, there was no answer to that question, and all of a sudden, there was a surprise witness. And how did this tie in with the noise in the woods? Was the committee confused or trying to cover-up? Talk of a conspiracy surfaced once again. With anxious looks, everyone leaned forward in their chairs. All eyes focused on the center of the room. The slave lowered his head to stare at the floor and spoke in a hushed voice.

"My name is Robert, and I belong to Master Armstrong on

Kent Island. One night while working the fields, I was captured by British soldiers. We sailed down the bay to your river. On the night they attacked, I was on deck doing chores. I was near the captain when the officers returned from the shore. I heard everything. They had planned to attack from the northwest, but they were scared off by the drums. They didn't think they had enough soldiers to overcome, so they called back all of their soldiers, even the ones near the harbor.

The room exploded in a barrage of heated accusations.

"We told you it was drums and not cannon fire," someone shouted.

"It's them Negroes," another voice rang out. "What we have on our hands is a rebellion."

Trying to regain order, the chairman pounded his wooden gavel like a sledgehammer. Over and over, he slammed the table. He pounded and pounded until the head of the mallet broke off and shot across the room. One spectator ducked at the last second to avoid a direct hit between the eyes. The gallery laughed hysterically. By accident, the comical mishap did what the chairman could not. The crowd quieted.

"Gentlemen," the chairman announced calmly, straightening his jacket, "There appears to be some truth in what Mr. Robert has said. Our commanders confirm there were no soldiers positioned in the north woods. As a result, the committee has decided all slave owners in the region will inquire, by whatever means necessary, to determine the involvement of their slaves in this matter. The board will convene in two days. This meeting is adjourned."

In the streets, the air was electric. Heated debate raged on every corner. The chairman's announcement only fueled the fire about a Negro uprising. Master Steele was remarkably composed as he left the building. To him, the answer was obvious. His plantation was closest to the woods. He knew what must be done.

When Steele returned home that afternoon, he immediately called for Hunt. Minutes later Hunt emerged from the manor house and assembled the slaves.

"Looks like we'll find out about that town meeting," Joseph said to Moses as they waited. Suddenly from around the corner,

Steele appeared and stepped up on the wood crate which served as a platform. He looked grim.

"I bring you good news," he said with a forced smile. "The town of St. Michael's has been saved. Thanks to a group of patriots who hid in the north woods, the British have been defeated. It appears they were frightened away by drummers. The town would like to reward these heroes. If you were involved, please step forward and be recognized for your bravery."

The slaves stood like stone pillars, their eyes squarely fixed on Master Steele.

"Your silence is understandable, but do not be afraid," Steele cajoled. "I will let you think about it. Remember, your reward will be quite handsome."

"I know of only a handful of drummers from the other plantations," Moses said to Joseph as Steele departed.

"It's obvious that Steele thinks the drummer is here," Joseph replied. With those words, terror filled his heart. The idea that Moses could be the drummer was ludicrous. He was asleep in the loft the night of the attack.

Moses saw the worried look on his father's face but said nothing. He knew what his father was thinking. Could they possibly suspect that Moses was the shadow drummer? About ten minutes later, Steele returned. A hardened scowl replaced the twisted smile.

"I will ask you again. If you have knowledge about the drumming, step forward." Again he was met with silence. "One last chance," he barked, now obviously annoyed. His eyes searched the group with disgust as he waited for an answer. "I will not have a rebellion of my slaves. This plantation is nearest to the woods. The drummers must be here," he shouted in anger. "If you won't give me an answer, I will be forced to get one."

Steele glanced over at Hunt and nodded his head. "Bring me King George," he ordered.

King George needed no escort. The proud slave walked to the front with a measured step like that of royalty. He was the last slave with direct ties to his homeland. Named after the British king during the Revolution, he incurred the eternal wrath of Master Steele. He was, and would be until his death, the defiant slave.

Claiming to be an African prince, he carried himself with

regal aplomb. He embraced his native customs and often spoke in his native tongue. No whip could silence him. Although he rarely socialized, he had the respect of every slave. He had the courage to defy the master.

"Tie him up," Steele ordered. Hunt and one of his henchman dragged George away and tied his arms between two posts. Sweat glistened on his back, highlighting a maze of scars which criss-crossed from his neck to his buttocks. Mister Hunt stepped off ten paces and uncoiled his bullwhip. He raised the whip behind his head and snapped it forward, exploding the hard dirt at the slave's heels. He reared back a second time. Slat! The tip of the whip bit into George's back like a viper. George stood triumphant with his arms outstretched. With each stroke, he bit down harder. There were no screams of pain, only the sound of leather striking flesh. Slat! Slit! Slat! After a few strokes, George lifted his head and stared hard into his master's cold blue eyes.

Moses was sick to his stomach. His head ached, and sweat poured from his face. He flinched with each stroke. When the whip tore open the scars and blood flowed down George's back, he turned away in shame. He was disgusted with himself. How could the grandson of Opatunji allow someone to be unjustly punished? He thought about Luther, and what Luther would do. He knew what must be done.

"Stop," he shouted, stepping to the front. "I'm the drummer."

Hunt dropped the whip to his side. Steele dropped his jaw to the ground. He was completely bewildered. The sudden admission caught him off guard. Bending down, he grabbed Moses by the chin and jerked it up to within a few inches of his own.

"Don't feel sorry for this dumb old Negro," he warned sharply. "If you're lying to me, I'll string you up next to him. If you're the drummer, you'll have to prove it."

Moses looked nervously at his father. "I, I, I have to get my drum," he stammered as he turned and ran to the edge of the woods. Joseph watched in sadness. He knew he would live to regret the day he promised to teach Moses about his heritage. All of this was his fault. Guilt flooded his heart. He knew the vengeance of the master was delivered with a deadly hand.

When Moses reached the trees, he thought about escaping. Looking back at the crowd, he quickly came to his senses. Even if he ran at full speed, he would be cornered by the dogs within an hour and torn to bits. Even if he did escape, his family would be punished in his place. He couldn't bear the thought of his father and mother tied up next to George. He was in a no-win situation. Hunt now had his chance for revenge. No doubt, he would be ruthless in its pursuit. The hourglass had finally run dry. Moses trotted back to Steele and handed him the drum. The interrogation began immediately.

"Where did you get the drum?" Steele asked.

Moses hesitated and looked at his father. "Go ahead Moses," he said. "Tell the truth." Joseph hoped that if Moses told the truth, Steele would vent his anger on him and not his son.

Moses paused. Should he lie to protect his father or should he tell the truth as his father instructed? Opatunji came to mind. "What would the master drummer do in a situation like this," he hurriedly asked himself. "Think! Think!" he told himself.

"I made the drum from a hollow log and dried goatskins," he declared boldly.

"And who helped you make the drum?"

"I made it by myself with tools from the stable."

"And where did you learn about such a drum?"

"Colonel Steele," Moses replied without hesitation.

"And when did Colonel Steele show you how to make an African drum?" Steele asked sarcastically, sure that Moses' alibi was unraveling.

"When the colonel visited the stables, he told stories about his days in the army. He talked about drummers leading the charge into battle. One day, he showed me a painting."

"And how did you know about the plans to defend the town?" Steele prodded in an attempt to trip up Moses.

"I overheard the colonel talking with militia leaders."

"You have all the right answers, especially since my father is so conveniently absent. But suppose everything you say is true, you still must prove this is your drum. To prove it, you must play it." Steele handed the drum to Moses. "Play like you did the night of the attack."

Moses stepped back and looped the drum around his neck. He turned the drum sideways and played every cadence he knew. He gradually increased the tempo, and in a few minutes, his fingers and hands raced across the drumheads in a blur. The drum thundered across the plantation. Steele closed his eyes and listened. After Moses finished, he closely examined the drum.

"Who taught you how to play the drum?" Steele asked.

"I taught myself," Moses said casually.

"I believe him," interrupted Hunt. "It's in their blood."

"Mister Hunt's right, master. It comes natural; just like the musicians at the Christmas frolic," Moses added as he breathed a sigh of relief. He looked at Steele who just stared at the drum and nodded his head. Unknowingly, Hunt had just rescued his sworn enemy. Moses didn't know how much longer he could have held up under the intense questioning.

"I believe you are the drummer," said Steele, satisfied by the performance. "I don't know exactly how, but you did it. Now it's time for one last performance. This time I'll have the honor."

Taking the drum, he lifted it over his head and slammed it to the ground. He then stomped the shell with his heel until it collapsed. Bending down, he picked up the mangled pile of wood and tossed it in the campfire. The fire hissed and flared for a second or two. A billowing cloud of white smoke drifted to the sky. "As promised," Steele said with a grin. "You shall have your reward."

When the committee reconvened two days later, the hoopla over the hearing had vanished. Empty chairs lined the hall. Street corners were deserted. Despite the furor at the end of the last meeting, interest waned with the passing of time.

"Gentlemen!" the chairman uttered in a tired voice. "Let's get to the point and finish the inquiry. Does anyone have anything to report?"

Master Steele rose from his seat. "I have found your Negro rebellion," he announced candidly. "Your drummer is a slave on my plantation named Moses. I assure you he is the one we are looking for. My overseer and I can attest to his drumming skills. Indeed, he is a quite primitive, but a remarkable musician."

"What are you going to do with your Negro?" one of the

other planters asked. "If we have Negroes going back to their tribal ways, we'll never get any work out of them."

"You must make an example of him. Trade, sell, or put him in the pillory for all to see, especially the other slaves," chimed in one of the committee members.

"Mister Steele," addressed the chairman. "The committee agrees that you must administer punishment to avoid this type of incident in the future."

With those words, a chorus of suggestions hailed from the small gathering. In the midst of the debate, Steele strode unnoticed to the center of room. There he tugged at his jacket lapels and cleared his throat rather loudly. This bold theatrical move caught everyone by surprise. Throughout the inquiry, Steele waited for his chance to upstage his fellow businessmen. Now was the time to strut his business savvy. For years, he heard the talk behind his back. He was merely born with a silver spoon in his mouth and rode his father's coattails into the family business. He wanted to end that nonsense once and for all. He was equal to, if not better than, any man in the room.

"Yes, gentlemen," said Steele coyly. "We must take action. However, your course is entirely wrong. The slaves do not need a martyr, they need a hero. Give them incentive to work. Showing them loyalty to their masters is in their best interests. Reward the boy for his bravery."

"Reward him with what? The title of militia commander," joked a committee member.

"It's not as ridiculous as you think. I have called upon a debt owed to my family. Arrangements will be made to send the boy to Baltimore. He will be assigned to the garrison at Fort McHenry. At the end of the war, he will be returned. I think you will find this a most favorable proposition."

"He's your property," said the chairman. "Although we can't tell you what to do with your holdings, I believe we all agree with your course of action."

"Thank you, gentlemen," Steele concluded. "I believe our hero will be departing within the week. Just as soon as the details of the transaction can be finalized."

That evening Moses was summoned to the manor house

where Steele gave him the news. Moses accepted it with quiet resignation. His one feeble plea to remain with his family was interrupted with an order not to discuss the matter any further. Moses was reminded to be thankful not resentful. After all, this was a reward for bravery.

Moses burst through the cabin door and ran into the arms of his mother. "Master Steele is making me leave," he sobbed. "I don't want to be a drummer. I want to be a stable boy." After telling his story to his parents, he sat dejectedly by the fireplace. Joseph and Martha were surprised but not shocked. They were relieved that Moses was not going to be sold outright. At Fort McHenry, he had a chance of someday returning to the plantation.

"You have to look at the bright side," said Joseph. "You're getting off the plantation. I've been stuck here my whole life; never seen anything else. Things can't be any worse there. You wanted to be a drummer, now is your chance. What do you think Luther would do? And besides, I hear the army treats its servants well. There's plenty of good food, a soft bed, and even time off."

"You're right, Papa," Moses lamented. "I have no other choice." His father's words did little to ease his worries.

That night, Moses slept in the cabin. One last time, he closed his eyes and listened to the lullaby of the plantation. With each breath, his body lightened. Link by link, he shed his chains of bondage which weighed him down. Finally free, he drifted to a faraway place in his dreams, a strange land he had never seen. He stood on a riverbank watching the sky. Overhead a black eagle glided on the thermals. The bird made several sweeping turns then plummeted to the river. Three times the eagle splashed the surface. Each time it came away with nothing but water dripping from its talons. After the last attempt, the eagle soared over the horizon and vanished into the clouds.

"It's time to go. The boat sails with the tide," Joseph announced at the morning's first light.

"Ready in a minute," Moses responded flatly. The night passed all too quickly. He took a last look around the cabin and turned toward his mother. He wanted to remember every detail about the place that had been his home for almost fourteen years.

"Take this for your trip," she said, handing him a small package wrapped in brown paper. "It's a little something I baked this morning." She clutched Moses to her chest. "Just remember, I love you. You'll always be in my thoughts," she whispered as tears streamed down her cheeks. "Whenever you're feeling lonely, I want you to think about your family. We've had some hard times here, but we always have a lot of love. Use that love to carry you through the hard times down the road."

"I'm afraid, Mama," Moses cried softly. "I'm afraid I'll never see you again."

His mother kissed him on both cheeks. "Always remember where you came from, and you'll have no trouble finding your way home. Now hurry! Your father's waiting."

Moses climbed aboard the wagon and sat next to his father. As the wagon rumbled passed the last field, the slaves stopped working. Like a legion of ghosts, they stood with blank stares. Their dusty faces shone like lifeless masks. From the back of the group, a lone voice began to croon a soft, mournful tune. One by one, the others joined until a great voice filled the air with song. They sung with a spirit that rose from far beneath the ground and soared to the mountaintops.

"What are they singing?" Moses asked.

"An old Negro spiritual," Joseph replied. "They're praising God for your good fortune and asking him for your safe deliverance."

The ride to St. Michael's was agonizing and slow. Over the years, Joseph made the trip a thousand times. Only today, he was delivering the most precious cargo he had ever carried. He was sending his son to an unknown fate. He wanted to talk, but he couldn't find the right words. When the rooftops of the town finally appeared, he tried to ease his pain. He still believed all of this was his fault.

"You know you did the right thing when you confessed to Master Steele the way you did," Joseph said. "You saved everyone a lot of suffering."

"But I lied," Moses protested weakly. "I should have done what I was taught. I wanted to do what the African drummer would have done, but I failed."

"One day you will learn what you did was honorable. Sometimes a lie is just another way of telling the truth."

They entered the edge of town and moved along main street. The business district was bustling with activity. As the wagon passed, the townspeople and storekeepers stopped and stared. A few blocks from the dock, Joseph and Moses heard the first shot.

"Don't say nothing," Joseph muttered under his breath. "Keep your eyes straight ahead." Seconds later another loud crack rang out, followed by another and then another. Suddenly Joseph summoned the courage to turn his head. A faint smile came to his face. People lined the streets and applauded their hero.

"Now, this is what I call a hero's welcome," Joseph whispered. "They're cheering for you, Moses."

Moses managed a tight-lipped smile. He bowed his head and shifted his eyes from side to side. He couldn't believe he was a hero. If he was such a hero, why wouldn't they let him stay on the plantation. The wagon finally creaked to a stop at the waterfront.

"Ahoy, Joseph! Waiting for your passenger," greeted a familiar voice.

"Just give us a minute, Captain," Joseph replied. He crouched down and grabbed Moses by the shoulders. "Be proud of who you are," he said looking Moses straight in the eye. "You are a worthy successor to the African drummer. The magic of the drum will always be with you as long as you believe in its power."

"I'll always remember," Moses said as he kissed his father. "And I want you to always remember, you did the right thing by teaching me the ways of our people." Moses dragged his feet to the end of the pier where he was greeted by a hearty handshake.

"Welcome aboard the Catherine Louise. Captain Christopher at your service," said the short, stocky man with a trimmed, gray beard that ran from ear to ear. "Have the run of the ship and make yourself comfortable. We'll be sailing hard to Baltimore. If you need anything, just holler."

The mooring lines were cast away and the two main sails hoisted into place. The schooner turned in the light breeze and headed for open water. Moses looked back at the pier and waved at the shrinking figure of his father.

Taking a seat near the bow, he watched glumly as land faded

from view. The thoughts of his family were as close as ever. In his heart, he knew he would never see them again. He was a slave, a piece of property to be bought and sold like the crates that were stacked on deck. He thought about Luther's mad dash across the bay. His bid for freedom cost him his life. He wondered how much more his freedom would cost before he paid for it with his own life. It had already cost him his family. "Is there anything left?" he muttered to himself in despair. With those words, he realized he had been betrayed by his owner. His reward was only a prolonged punishment.

Moses looked around the deck. He wondered if these sights and sounds were the ones his grandfather experienced when he sailed on the slave ship. A warm spray splashed his face as the graceful lady sliced through the waves. Overhead, musty canvas sails snapped smartly in the wind. The brown dirt of the plantation field was a rolling carpet of emerald green water. The smell of horse sweat and manure was now a perfume of pitch and pine. Moses quickly discovered what sailors had known for hundreds of years. The sea was good therapy for a heavy heart.

"Come about to port," came the order as the schooner tacked to enter the mouth of the Patapsco River. Land once again appeared on both sides of the ship.

Captain Christopher made his way to the bow and tapped Moses on the shoulder. "Look straight ahead. There's your new home."

On a piece of land splitting the river, Moses saw a long, red, brick wall and black rooftops. Centered, was a tall flag pole which flew a banner of red and blue. An hour later, the schooner docked. Moses was delivered to a young soldier waiting at the end of the pier.

"Here's your cargo or should I say recruit," Christopher joked. "Take good care of the boy or I'll drown you in bilge water."

"Welcome to Fort McHenry," the soldier chuckled. "Gather your belongings and follow me."

Chapter Eight—

The Heart of the City

Moses leaned forward to climb the hill which led to the fort. His steps were painfully short. The long hours of sitting had tightened his muscles. It took him some time to walk off his sea legs. As he approached the sally port, the main gate, he stepped alongside his escort with a smooth, confident stride. Passing under the archway, he was dwarfed by the massive twelve-foot walls. He wasn't scared, just nervous about his new home. He would follow his father's advice and make the best of the situation. After crossing a small parade field, he entered the commander's office.

"Yes, corporal," said the soldier, hovered over some papers on his desk. "I see you standing there."

"Sir. Delivering your cargo from the afternoon packet."

"Stand at ease. I'll be right with you," came the reply without a glance. "It takes a mountain of paperwork to buy a flag. But we certainly don't want to upset Mrs. Pickersgill by being late with our payment." After jotting some notes in his ledger, the officer laid down his quill and looked up. "You must be Mr. Moses from St. Michael's."

"Yes, sir. Just arrived on the schooner," Moses replied.

"I'm Major George Armistead, commander at Fort McHenry. I'll be honest with you from the start. You were accepted as a political favor. I do not desire young boys in my unit. However, while you are here, you will be put to good use. You will be under my charge during your stay. I expect you to obey all the rules just as the other soldiers. Now let's take care of your paperwork.

"Last name?"

"None, sir."

"Age?"

"I believe thirteen going on fourteen, sir."

"Occupation."

"Sir, what's an occupation?"

"Your skill or trade. Something you know how to do."

Moses collected his thoughts. He saw his chance. No use in being bashful with a bunch of strangers, he thought. With just the right word, he could fulfill the dream of a lifetime.

"Drummer boy, sir."

"Any experience?"

"Yes, sir, but only a little," Moses said reluctantly. The question caught him off guard.

"Any other skill?"

"I worked in Master Steele's stable," replied a dejected Moses, sensing his opportunity had been lost.

"You'll report to Sergeant MacDonald. He'll assign you to your duties."

Moses followed his escort across the parade field to one of the two-story brick barracks. Standing outside the door was a giant of a man with red hair and a thick beard that blazed in the sunlight.

"Glad to meet you, lad," the soldier bellowed in a thick Scottish accent. "I'm Sergeant Ian MacDonald of the MacDonald clan from the highlands of Scotland. But you can call me Sergeant Mac."

"Moses from St. Michael's," Moses said meekly, extending his hand. After a brief interview, Moses got his first assignment. In this man's army, experience would not be wasted.

"We'll start you in the stables with one of my best men," Sergeant Mac announced. "Whatever you need, let me know. Come along now. I'll give you the grand tour."

The rest of the afternoon Moses followed in the sergeant's footsteps. After dinner, he left the sergeant and climbed the fort's walls for a better look at his new home. Outside the fort stood storehouses, a hospital, and the stable. Inside the walls were the barracks, the armory, and the guardhouse. Everywhere he looked he saw red. A million, a billion, a trillion bricks, he thought. From his perch, he saw the five points of the star fort which jutted out from the corners. Cannons mounted on heavy wooden carriages pointed downriver.

Bone-tired from the longest day in his life, Moses sat on the wall and tried to relax. He cocked his head and listened. This was the beginning of a new life with new rhythms. The flag fluttered in the light breeze, its lines smacking against the pole. In the distance, the din of the city echoed in the evening. Around the bend in the river was the bustling seaport of Baltimore. He heard many tales about the city, but he never imagined he would get so close. Some slaves said that you could buy your freedom there. Moses didn't know how it could be done, since slaves didn't have any money, but the story offered hope. So close to his dreams, but still a thousand miles away, he thought.

If Luther could only see him now. He wasn't quite a regimental drummer, but he had made it across the Chesapeake. Folding his shirt into a pillow, he rested his head. He closed his eyes and hoped to dream about his family. He prayed the fort wasn't a dream. He was pleased with the turn of events. All things considered, his first day away from home went well.

The crack of the drum sounding reveille shattered the morning stillness. Moses threw on his shirt and ran down to the barracks. Soldiers already stood in formation.

"Over here lad," Sergeant Mac called out. "I want you to meet Private Sharkey. For the time being, you'll be working for him. By the way, where did you sleep last night?"

"On the wall, sir."

"That's fine if you're a pigeon, but if you work for me, you sleep in my barracks."

"Yes, sir!" Moses responded with a snappy hand salute.

"Don't be calling me sir," Mac replied with a chuckle. "That's for officers only. I earned my rank just like every man around here."

Sharkey handed Moses an old uniform shirt and pants. Without bothering to change, he slipped them over his old clothes. Though baggy and worn, they made him look like a soldier. More importantly, they made him feel like one. Moses desperately wanted to blend with his new surroundings. He wanted to belong to the fort

Only seventeen years old, Sharkey displayed a compassion and wisdom beyond his years. It was easy to see why Sergeant Mac had so much faith in him. All he needed to become a good soldier was experience. Mac was giving him his chance. Sharkey had never been in charge of anyone or anything. Moses was his first command. It was a challenge for both. Sharkey's orders were more like pleas for mercy which never failed to amuse Moses.

"Moses! I want you to polish the saddles for inspection or Sergeant Mac will give me extra duty. If you don't mind."

"Yes sir," Moses replied sharply. To boost Sharkey's confidence, Moses always wore a serious look when receiving his orders. He didn't dare let Sharkey know he liked him. Sharkey knew his way around pots and pans, but knew nothing about saddles and stirrups. For that reason, Moses was left by himself to run the stable. With ten horses to clean and feed, his day was busy. The work was the same as on the plantation except now he had a bed, three meals a day, a uniform and no overseer.

After a few days on the job, the routine became boring, just like back on the plantation. Moses could handle the work but not the loneliness. More than anything in the world, he wished he had someone to talk with. Sharkey and Sergeant Mac stopped by a couple of times a day to check on things, but they quickly went about their business. If only Luther was around, he thought, then things would be fun.

"Psst! Psst!" came a hissing sound. Moses raised his pitchfork and stabbed at the piles of straw. He had seen rats the size of rabbits scurrying around the feed bins. "Psst! Psst!" There it was again, only this time louder. The sound seemed to move along the wall. Moses lunged again and missed the varmint by inches. He lifted the pitchfork and froze. The intruder was an old brown shoe.

"The name is Henry Bremmendorf," the visitor said. "And you must be Moses?"

"I am Private Moses of the United States Army," Moses replied sternly. "And you, sir, are trespassing on government property."

"Didn't mean to scare you," Henry apologized. "Don't worry. Sergeant Mac told me all about you. I'm from the orphanage up the road. I spend most of my free time around the fort. It's my home away from home. Mostly, I run errands for Sergeant Mac.

He said I could enlist in his unit when I'm old enough. I'll be twelve in a couple of months." Henry paused to catch his breath and then extended his hand. "Pleased to meet you. If I can ever be of help, just let me know."

"If you want to help, there's plenty to do around here," Moses replied, waving his hand around the stable. He hoped Henry would at least stay for a few minutes and talk. Without another word, Henry grabbed a pitchfork and began tossing straw.

"I see you met my friend Henry, the tunnel rat of Fort McHenry," MacDonald bellowed as he entered the stable. "He knows more about the fort than the man who designed it. He's a good man, Moses. Listen to him. He knows his way around here."

After Sergeant Mac left, Henry picked up the conversation.

"Been to the city?"

"No. I've been here only a week," Moses replied. "Don't know if I can leave the fort. The major told me I have to obey all the rules, but I'm not really in the army so I . . . "

"I know all of that," Henry interrupted. "Sergeant Mac said you were a slave from down on the shore. Well, you're not on a plantation and you're not in the army, so to me it looks like you somewhere in between. And when you're in between, you can pretty much go in any direction you want. So what do you say? Ready for your first liberty, soldier?"

Moses hesitated. He didn't want to disobey orders, but he had to admit he was lonely. Henry's offer was tempting. He certainly didn't want to lose a friend. Finally, his sense of adventure overcame his fear. And besides, Henry's argument was enough to convince anyone, he reasoned. If caught, he hoped it would be enough to convince Major Armistead.

"When do we go?" he asked.

"I'll meet you here after dark."

Minutes after the sun fell behind the trees, Henry was standing outside the stable. Moses wondered if he suddenly materialized out of thin air or stood outside since the afternoon. Either way, Henry was good on his word. After a quick rundown on the night's trip, the pair headed toward the city. They followed the main road for about a mile and then headed downhill to the harbor. Henry led the way through a maze of dark alleys. Like a mouse, he darted around buildings and sprinted across deserted streets. After an endless number of twists and turns, they arrived at the water's edge.

Moses was instantly captivated. The waterfront was still alive with activity. Everywhere, men scurried along wharves hauling cargo, stopping only to wipe the sweat from their faces. Wagons lined up next to the warehouses, waiting to load barrels of raw sugar and coffee. Every pier was crowded with sailing vessels, two and three abreast. The air was thick with the smell of wet canvass, damp hemp, and freshly cut wood. Moses inhaled this exotic aroma. He was under the spell of a river and loving every minute.

Working their way around the harbor basin, they passed underneath the red cliffs of Federal Hill then headed for the shipbuilding community of Fell's Point on the opposite side. On the return trip, the warehouses and shipyards were quiet. Workers had moved indoors. Stevedores and sailors spilled from the taverns which stood on every street corner. Through the swinging doors, Moses saw men drinking, arguing, gambling and singing in a sea of stale beer and sweat. Their loud voices spoke many strange tongues. To his surprise, Moses even saw a group of black men gathered inside one of the public houses.

On the way home, Henry stopped in an alley behind a large stone building which looked more like a factory than a house. "This is where I live. I'll have to sneak in or else I'll get paddled. You shouldn't have any trouble finding your way back. Just follow the alley until you reach the dirt road. Turn left and it will take you right to the fort."

Just as quickly as Henry appeared outside the stable, he disappeared through the cellar window. Moses took off running, hoping he could remember his way back. When he reached the grassy fields surrounding the fort, he crouched low to avoid being seen by the sentries atop the walls. He was glad he convinced Sergeant Mac to let him sleep in the stable. This way he could come and go as he pleased. And besides, he wanted to stay in the stable for sentimental reasons. A loft, any loft, was his home away from home. It reminded him of his family back on the plantation.

That evening Moses laid on his straw bed and closed his

eyes, but he was too excited to sleep. "I must go back," he mumbled over and over. "There is so much to see." The image of the black men in the tavern crowded his mind. The next day, he was shocked to learn from Sergeant Mac that they were former slaves who bought their freedom while working at the shipyards. They were now shipwrights who earned a wage for their labor. To Moses, they were simply free men, regardless of where they worked or what they did. Freedom was close at hand, just up the road. Maybe, one day he could buy his freedom, he thought.

Henry and Moses toured the waterfront every week. When the headmaster punished Henry by locking him in his room at night, Moses made the trip alone. His only destination was the shipyard near the red cliffs. It became an obsession. Nothing could stop him from exploring this new world. Even Henry's stories about free blacks being kidnapped off the streets in daylight and "sold South" for up to $5,000.00 failed to stop him.

Moses found a trusty hiding spot in a tree overlooking the harbor. He watched and waited in the darkness. When he was sure the last worker was gone for the day, he vaulted over the wall in the blink of an eye. Once inside, he walked among the giant oak skeletons and marveled at the skill it took to build a boat. Every trip bolstered his hopes. He was sure that one day he could get a job in the shipyard. Then it would be just a matter of time until he saved enough money to buy his freedom. His future was in shipbuilding, not drumming.

By fall, life at the fort had settled into a rather dull but predictable routine. The stable was always busy. Moses still made the trips by himself and Henry only came around on the weekends. He was a welcomed visitor since the fort was deserted on the weekends as most of the soldiers were on liberty. The place could be very depressing when you were by yourself. One Saturday in November, Mrs. Pickersgill and her daughter Caroline visited the fort to repair the mammoth battle flag they had delivered in August. With the help of Henry and Moses, they unfolded the flag and reinforced the stitching on the stars.

The flag was a marvel. It covered nearly a quarter of the parade field, measuring forty-two feet by thirty feet. It held fifteen white stars, eight red stripes and seven white ones. Each star was twenty-six inches from point to point, and each stripe was twenty-four inches wide. Mrs. Pickersgill closely inspected every inch of threading. When she came to a weak stitch, she adroitly threaded a new one with her oversized needle. Her calloused fingers operated with the skill of a surgeon.

"Come here, Moses," she called. "I'll show you how it's done."

"But I don't know how to sew. And besides, I don't want to ruin your flag," replied Moses politely.

"Nonsense. This flag belongs to everyone," she gently chided.

Moses placed two stitches in one of the stars before stabbing his finger. A pinpoint of blood stained the blue field holding the stars.

"Fine job," Mrs. Pickersgill exclaimed when he had finished. "We can't have states falling from the Union before the flag is ever flown," she chuckled.

Moses took advantage of the short days and long nights by visiting the waterfront at least twice a week. Within a couple of weeks, he had made the trip so many times he could do it blindfolded. Like Luther, he was one with the night.

The arrival of cold weather in December abruptly ended his tours. When the temperature dipped below freezing, Sergeant Mac ordered him to sleep in the barracks. His request for a couple of wool blankets was denied. He was trapped inside the walls. Escape was impossible. The shipyard was out of the question. With the holiday season rapidly approaching, Moses decided to relax and enjoy his first Christmas away from home.

Unlike the hectic pace of the plantation, Christmas at the fort was the slowest time of the year. With the British fleet retreating to the lower reaches of the bay until spring, soldiers had plenty of time on their hands. To boost morale, leave was encouraged. As a result, the fort was empty for the holiday.

Christmas Day was celebrated with a holiday feast. Soldiers who stayed behind prepared a lavish dinner in the early afternoon. The rest of the day was spent around the fireplace drinking ale. After a round or two of hearty toasts, Sergeant Mac handed out small gifts.

"And last but not least, we have something for our youngest recruit," he announced. Step forward and accept your gift, lad."

Moses ripped open the package. Underneath the wrapping paper was a custom-crafted, eight-inch hunting knife with a bone handle.

"Hope you like it," Mac said.

"Never had anything like it," Moses replied. "Slaves couldn't own any weapons. Matter of fact, slaves couldn't own anything."

"Well, you're not on the plantation anymore. Before I forget, let me give you the important news. I saw Captain Christopher the other day. He spoke to your father about a week ago. Your family is fine and everyone sends their love. I told the captain to tell him you're doing well. Plenty of hard work and good friends."

"I don't know what to say other than thanks," Moses said humbly. He was touched by everyone's kindness. Only a few months ago, he was a perfect stranger to the unit, and a slave boy at that.

"That's good enough, lad. And one more thing. Don't forget the pots and pans," Mac added with a belly laugh.

Moses went right to work. By the time he finished, the barrack was empty. The men had taken their celebration into town. Moses was alone and lonely. To cheer himself up, he decided to walk the wall. In the past, it was the perfect tonic to cure those homesick blues.

Moses searched the river for a sign of life. Not a ship or person was in sight. Soft ice was beginning to form along the riverbank. The landscape was dreary and desolate. So much for the cheering up, he thought. He tried a different approach and reflected on this Christmas Day. Indeed, it had been a grand holiday. Only one thing could make it better. "The shipyard," he said to himself. "I'll have the whole place to myself." No need to sneak pass the guards. By now, they knew who he was and let him pass without a challenge.

Moses ran along his route. Every second was precious. Tonight there was no chance of being caught by the constable. It was Christmas. The streets were deserted. Everyone was home with their families. Glancing over both shoulders, he climbed the wall and walked to the water's edge. Even in the winter, work at the yard continued. A number of ships were out of the water and cradled on blocks. Moses climbed ladders and scaffolding. He poked around the piles of junk and peered into windows of the work sheds. All of the time, he searched for some clue to the identities of the black men who worked there.

"Now I got you," the attacker shouted. Moses felt a thick, powerful arm reach around his neck and lift him off the ground. "Move a muscle and I'll break you in two." The man slowly released his grip and spun Moses around. Moses trembled with fear. A face as black as coal looked him in the eyes. He had seen most, if not all, of the men at the yard. This was a face he didn't recognize.

"Look what I caught here," said the stranger, equally surprised to see a black face staring back. "A runaway slave! This must be my lucky day."

"No! No!" Moses cried out, fearing he was about to be kidnapped. "I'm with the soldiers at the fort. I'm on loan from a plantation at St. Michael's. I tend the horses. My commander is Major..."

"That's enough. If I don't believe you, you'll talk my ears off," the man replied impatiently. "Who are you and what business do you have here?"

"I'm Moses, just plain old Moses from Fort McHenry. I came to see the men who work here and find out how they got their freedom."

"The name's Frederick Hart, master carpenter at the yard," the stranger said in a friendlier tone. "If you're looking for freedom, tonight might be your lucky night. But you won't find it here. Let's go to my house for a cup of hot tea. We'll talk there. It's only a few blocks from here."

Moses walked a step behind the stranger, still leery of his intentions. "Are you are a free man?" he asked.

"As free as the birds in the sky. Well, not quite that free. No one owns me, if that's what you mean. I don't own much, but I do own this house," Hart said, opening the door to the narrow, brick row house. Hart lit a candle and invited Moses to sit in the parlor. For the next hour, Moses talked and Hart listened as Moses recalled his journey from the plantation to the fort. When he spoke about becoming a drummer, Hart's ears perked up with a keen interest.

"So you want to be a drummer?" Hart asked spiritedly. "Then follow me. I have something you might like to see."

Moses followed Hart to the second floor. He stood in the dark hallway as Hart began lighting candles in one of the rooms. Within minutes, the room was ablaze in the light of a hundred candles.

"My drum hut," Hart said proudly, waving his hand around the room. Moses was dumbstruck. Drums of every shape and size filed the room—cone drums, cylinder drums, long drums, barrel drums, goblet drums, waisted drums, footed drums with carved animal feet, and kettledrums. To compliment the drums and the decor, hand carved tribal masks covered the walls. Long, oval faces, painted in white, red, black and green, stared at the drums like ghostly sentries. The flickering light streaked their savage faces. They appeared to be alive.

"Please forgive the heat," Hart said. "But the spirits of the drums require warmth." As Moses looked around, he noticed the bed which was set up like an altar. On it stood two barrel drums with bulging and brooding red eyes fixed on the entrance to the room. At the foot of the bed, a bowl of milk was offered to nourish the spirits who occupied the drums.

"In his native land, my father was a young man who studied to become a master drummer," Hart continued. "He was sent to this country in the chains. Before he died, he taught me all he could about his people. He tried to teach me the ways of the master drummer, but I was too young at the time. Now that I am older, I collect stories from the slaves I meet at the docks. In the carpenter's shop, I make the drums they describe to me. I have the knowledge, yet I am powerless to call upon the spirits. While I have many talents in life, I was not blessed with the spirit of the drummer. What I need is a willing student. Would you like to share my knowledge?"

Moses was startled by Hart's offer. He had little time to think. In the back of his mind, he was still afraid he would be kidnapped. The wrong answer might seal his fate. "I would like to visit again," he replied hesitantly. While he was too frightened to say no, he had to admit he was fascinated by Hart and his drum hut.

"Fine. We'll meet here next week," said a delighted Hart.

After Moses left, Hart grabbed a drum from his bed and began tapping a short, rhythmic cadence. He looked at the masks and chanted a prayer in his native tongue. The flames on the candles surged upward with a sudden energy. Mysterious shadows danced about the room. The masks came to life, their empty eyes filled with a fiery glow. "Perhaps, I have found the spirit of the drummer in the spirit of this Christmas," he thought. "Maybe, just maybe, the long wait is over." A wide smile stretched across his face. This was his lucky day. This year his gift would be in giving.

Chapter Nine—

Drumming in the Ranks

Through the long winter months, Moses visited the drum hut every week. Frederick talked endlessly about drums and drummers, while Moses constantly asked questions about carpenters and the shipyards. Despite his casual attitude toward the lessons, Moses learned more than he ever knew about drumming. Frederick taught him about each drum in the room. He even demonstrated the ritual for consecrating a drums. To him, it was the most important lesson. For without it, the drum was only a chunk of wood. Each step had to be carefully followed. Only then was the drum a sacred instrument to call on the gods.

When the weather warmed, the visits became sporadic. The British were sailing up the Chesapeake with a larger fleet. Every town along the bay was preparing for war. Moses, still living in the fort, was unable to sneak away. Hart was disappointed but understood the needs of the army. He was more determined than ever to see his student graduate.

To prepare for the final visit, Hart read the hundreds of slave stories he had collected over his lifetime. He diligently took notes, searching for the special bond between drum and drummer. Somewhere in his stories, he hoped to find the key which unlocked the door to the secrets of the master drummer. From sundown to sunup, he labored in the drum hut by the light of a hundred candles. Moses was ready for life's journey, and Hart had to give him a gift that would guide him for a lifetime.

When Moses arrived, Frederick was ready. He took a barrel drum and held it over his head with its eyes looking down at

Moses. "The drum is a circle like the sun and the moon. Each has its own power. You, as the master drummer, can bring these forces of the universe together. Your grandfather died without his sacred drum, and now his spirit walks the earth. One day, you will be able to free his spirit through the drum," he declared.

"But how will I know his spirit sits with the owner of heaven?" Moses asked.

"The drum will give you the answer. It will talk to you in ways you can never imagine."

"But I have no drum."

"You have the knowledge of the drummer. One day, you will find the drum to call upon the gods. When it has been baptized by fire and rain, it will be an instrument of infinite power."

"But what if I decide I do not want to be a drummer?"

"Remember, you are blessed with a special talent. You will never be free until you free the spirit of your ancestor."

"But what if my freedom is found in the shipyard?" Moses pleaded, hoping Hart would finally see things his way.

"There are many forks along the road to freedom. You must choose the one which is right for you. The drum will help you choose. It is truth and courage. It is the heartbeat of freedom. Never be blinded by your shortcomings that you fail to see these virtues."

It was after midnight when Moses left the house. He carefully stalked the streets. It would be months, maybe never, before he saw Hart again. He didn't want to be caught on the last trip. In the wee hours of a Sunday morning, the taverns were still packed with hard-working and hard-drinking men. At the last saloon before the fort, he heard a familiar voice rise above the others.

"Come on, lad. Put up your dukes. I'll teach you a lesson about cheating at cards," the man shouted.

Moses turned the corner and peered down the alley. Sergeant Mac stood with his hands at his chin, preparing to engage in a bout of fisticuffs. Without warning, his opponent lunged with a right hand. Mac fended off the blow with a forearm and delivered a hard fist to the stomach. The man doubled over in pain as air raced from his lungs.

"I'll kill you. You stinking sheepherder," the man barked,

lunging again at Mac from a kneeling position. This time the sergeant's fist landed squarely on the chin. As the man fell to the ground in a crumpled heap, his two henchman, who had been standing nearby, joined the fray. They grabbed Mac and pinned his arms behind his back. His opponent slowly rose to his feet and wiped the blood from the corners of his mouth. He cocked his fist and delivered a blow to the jaw. The punch snapped back Mac's head. "Now it's my turn to teach a lesson," the man yelled. He delivered another blow, then stooped down to pick up a board.

Moses watched from the shadows, afraid to even breathe. When he saw the man reach to the ground, he rushed forward and kicked the assailant squarely in the groin. A follow-up knee to the chest toppled him backwards. Like a tiger, Moses pounced on his wounded prey. In one swift motion, he pulled his knife from its sheath and held it across the man's throat.

"Now let the sergeant go," he screamed, his hand shaking with fear. "Or I'll cut your friend from ear to ear."

The men dropped the sergeant and scattered. The man on the ground scurried away like a rat. Sergeant MacDonald slowly rose to his feet and dusted off his uniform.

"Lad, I don't know where you came from, but you saved my life. I owe you a debt, and a good Scotsman always keeps his word."

The next morning Sergeant Mac, as usual, was standing outside the barracks bright and early. Except for a few nasty welts on his face, his night of carousing seemed to have had no ill effects. After formation, he ordered Moses to stand and be ready. He then walked over to the musicians across the parade ground and borrowed a drum.

"You want to be a drummer," he said, handing the drum to Moses. "Well, here's your chance. Let's hear you play."

Moses placed the sling around his neck and positioned the drum in alignment with his left leg. He placed the butt end of one drumstick in the web of his left hand next to his thumb and rested the shaft near the first knuckle of his ring finger. The grip felt awkward but that's how the regimental drummers did it. He had to show Sergeant Mac he at least looked like a real drummer. In fact, he had never in his life tried to play a drum in this manner.

He squeezed the other stick firmly in the palm of his right hand. The oversized oak drumsticks were cumbersome. Taking a deep breath to calm his nerves, he struck the drum with a quick right and left hand. Tump! Da-tump! The sticks bounced wildly off the drumhead. He returned the sticks to the starting position and tried again. Tump! Da-tump! A pained looked of frustration was etched across his face. He tried again and again. The results were the same.

Moses was frustrated. His chance of becoming a drummer was slipping away before his very eyes. His future was literally in his hands and he was helpless. Finally, he tossed the sticks to the ground and turned the drum on its side. He played the way he knew how. With his fingers, he sounded reveille and tattoo.

Da-rum-dum-dum-dum! Da-rum-dum-dum-dum! He started slowly with one beat at a time, then picked up the tempo until his fingers and hands moved like a whirlwind. As the volume increased, so did the attention. All eyes focused on the stable boy as he imitated every drum command, stroke for stroke. When his hands and arms finally tired, Moses brought the audition to an end with a thunderous slam. Applause filled the air. Moses didn't play like a regimental drummer but he sure sounded like one.

"I think there's some potential here," Sergeant Mac said with a chuckle. "I'll let you practice with the other drummers whenever I can. We can always use another drummer."

The opportunity to be a regimental drummer gave new life to Moses. For the time being, he forgot about building boats as a career. He spent every free hour practicing the rudiments of drumming on a block of wood, using a pair of homemade sticks. He quickly mastered the descriptive strokes of the flam, ruff, paradiddle and ratamacue. In a similar fashion, the drum commands for assembly, march, reveille, tattoo, call to arms and parley were polished in a matter of days. He remembered some of the commands from his days on the drill field with Colonel Steele. All the drum corps had to do was play the cadence once, and he had it memorized. Like magic, the drumsticks became a mere extension of his fingers.

One Saturday afternoon, Sergeant Mac called Moses over to his bunk.

"You made me see the evil of my ways. Too much drink does a man no good. So I'm quitting for now. Being a real Scotsman is not drinking a barrel of Scotch whisky but blowing the pipes," he said as he lifted the bagpipes to his chest. Moses was bewildered by the strange contraption. He watched as MacDonald cradled the leather bag with five protruding pipes and blew into the valve pipe. The instrument hummed and buzzed like a horde of locust. Ever so slowly, the most beautiful and haunting sounds emerged. The music was a mournful melody which recalled a mournful past. It reminded Moses of the song the slaves had sung on the morning he left the plantation.

"Come on, lad. Get your drum and let's play," Mac directed as he headed out the door. Once on the wall, they took positions facing each other. The sweet notes of the bagpipe paced by the cadence of the parade drum caught the breeze and drifted along the river. People on the city streets turned their ears to the melodious sounds. They instantly knew the crazy Scotsman had once again given up drinking.

More than music began filling the fort. Throughout the spring and summer, local militia units trained daily at the fort. From sunup to sundown, soldiers practiced battle formations in the grassy fields outside the walls. Inside, recruits marched in close order drill. More soldiers meant more practice time for Moses who was now an unofficial member of the Fort McHenry band. With the band and the stable, his days were more hectic than those on the plantation. Even Independence Day, the Fourth of July 1814, was a working holiday.

Sergeant Mac called the formation to attention and read the orders for the day. Afterward, Major Armistead addressed the troops.

"Mr. Moses, front and center," he ordered. Moses stood erect with his eyes fixed on the major's chest. He was puzzled by the sudden attention. He feared he was being sent back to the plantation.

"Attention to orders," the major bellowed. "By the power entrusted in me by the Governor of the State of Maryland, I, hereby, authorize Moses from the township of St. Michael's honorary enlistment to the rank of private in the Maryland Militia at Fort

McHenry. He is authorized to wear the military uniform of the garrison with all proper insignia and shall be accorded the military respect and courtesy accorded his rank."

Moses remained standing at attention, unable to move. His arms and legs were paralyzed by the news. I must be dreaming, he thought. He was a soldier and therefore an official member of the band. He was at last a regimental drummer. All it took was a piece of paper with a few simple words to fulfill his dream. Indeed, in the hands of the major, the pen was mightier than the sword. He wished his family could see him now. He knew Luther was watching proudly from up above.

The daydream was shattered by Sergeant Mac's booming voice.

"Don't stand there like a statue, soldier. Salute your commander."

"Thank you, sir," Moses said with a crisp hand salute.

"Don't thank me, private. Thank yourself," the major replied. "You worked hard. It's an honor to have a man like you in my unit."

After dinner, as the soldiers enjoyed their last cup of coffee, Sergeant MacDonald rose from his table and handed Moses a large, burlap bag. "From the men of the barracks. A sign of our appreciation."

Moses lifted the drum from the bag. At first, he failed to recognize the battered parade that he had borrowed. The plain, brown shell was painted a dark blue with a large black eagle centered on the front. On the eagle's chest was a shield of red and white stripes underneath a blue field imbedded with five white stars. In its beak, the eagle held a banner which read "Fort McHenry, Maryland, 1814. The pointed talons held a quiver of arrows and an olive branch. Above the eagle's head was an arching white cloud holding five gold stars. The brown flesh hoops were painted a brilliant red. Even the drumheads, tension ropes and black leather braces had been replaced. The colors were simply dazzling. The old drum had been transformed from a musical instrument into musical masterpiece.

"It's your drum now. You're the new owner," Mac said. "The men and I bought it from the quartermaster."

Moses glanced at the rough, weathered faces which were full of laughter. This was a side of the men he had never seen. A soldier's life was hard. The men took pride in their toughness. There was no room for emotions, much less a display of affection for a slave boy. Moses smiled with them. He swelled with pride. It felt good to be accepted for his contributions and not his color.

"I hope that I will prove worthy to own such a fine drum," Moses said sincerely.

"Don't worry, lad. You already have," replied Mac.

Moses carried the drum to his bunk where he studied its every detail. Over and over, he ran his fingers across the black eagle painted on the shell. He couldn't wait to show it to Henry and Frederick.

When he arrived at the orphanage, the building was dark. The children had not returned from their outing in the country. With no time to wait, he ran to Frederick's house. He knocked hard and entered through the back door. The house was hollow and cold like a cave.

"Frederick! Frederick!" he called out, but no one answered. He raced upstairs to the bedroom and stopped dead in his tracks. The drum hut was empty. Except for an old, broken bed in the corner, there was nothing; no drums, no masks and no Frederick. His eyes nervously searched the room. In the corner was a shallow bowl filled with milk and rice. Underneath the bowl was a black feather.

Moses picked up the offering and remembered Frederick's story about consecrating the drum. The signs were clear. He knew what must be done. As he left the house, an elderly woman across the street stood in her doorway and eyed him suspiciously.

"I'm looking for Frederick Hart, the man who lives here," Moses shouted.

"You must be mistaken, young man," the lady replied. "Ain't no one lived in that house for years. Last person to live there was a runaway slave. He was there for about a year until the bounty hunters found him. Murdered him in his sleep I heard."

"But I saw a man in this house," said a bewildered Moses.

"Maybe what you saw was a ghost. People say the house is haunted. Every year around this time, they say he comes back to find out if he's really dead or just dreaming. Some people claim they hear his screams in the night."

For some odd reason, Moses believed the woman's story. He knew he wasn't dreaming and didn't have any explanation for the appearance or disappearance of Frederick, the mystery man. Come to think of it, he never saw any carpenter's tools at Frederick's house. And Frederick's hands were not hard and calloused like someone who worked with wood. His hands were smooth and soft, almost cool to the touch. He rarely, if ever, talked about ships. It was always drums and drummers.

Moses hightailed it to shipyard. At the water's edge, he removed the drum from the bag.

"Olodumare, supreme being of the universe, I ask you to bless this drum in the name of Opatunji and Frederick. Give it life with their spirits," he said as he stepped into the river and gently splashed water over the shell.

"Olodumare, supreme being," he called out again. "I am Moses, a master drummer. Always protect this sacred drum. Accept this offering as a sign of my respect for your powers. Carry me upon the river of life to your shore where my ancestors wait."

Moses placed the bowl in the river and watched it drift away with the current. Next he brushed his body and then the drum with the feather and tossed it in the air. The feather floated downward in a lazy spiral. Right before it touched the water, a sudden burst of wind whipped across the harbor. The feather took flight to the heavens as if it had come to life. "Thank you, Olodumare," Moses whispered as he looked to the sky.

Chapter Ten—

The Rocket's Red Glare

On the morning of September 19th, the British fleet was sighted at the mouth of the Patapsco River. Da-rum! Da-rum-dum-dum! Dum-dum! Moses sounded the general alarm. Men raced to their battle stations. The Battle of Baltimore had begun.

The next morning in gusting winds and heavy showers, the warships closed on the fort and opened fire. The guns along the wall immediately responded with a heavy barrage. Throughout the day, the British played a cat and mouse, moving close to fire and retreating beyond range. Moses spent the day hauling gunpowder to the wall and fetching water for the gun batteries.

After a lull in the early evening, the British resumed the bombardment at midnight. Two hours later, when a landing force was spotted near the fort, an artillery duel to the death ensued. Moses reported to Sergeant Mac's battery for his orders. He was tired and sore, but revitalized at the prospect of working with a gun battery. Adrenalin coursed through his veins like liquid lightning.

Swoooosh! A bomb passed overhead with a thunderous roar. Standing near the 24-pound cannon, Moses cupped his hands over his ears. Seconds later, a second bomb found its target. Ka-bloom! With a deafening blast, the 190 pound bomb hammered the cannon, shattering the gun barrel and splintering the carriage. Bodies flew in the air like rag dolls. Moses was thrown to the ground and knocked unconscious. Coming to his senses, he crawled to the wreckage. Two of the gunners had been killed instantly, their bodies ripped apart by the shower of deadly shrapnel.

"Sergeant Mac! Sergeant Mac!" he called out in the smoky haze which shrouded the wall.

"Over here, lad," Mac moaned.

Moses found the sergeant on the other side of the gun circle. His face was streaked with black soot; his shirt and pants soaked with blood.

"I can't move my legs," he said painfully. "Now get away before they fire again. They've seen the explosion and marked our position. Save yourself. That's an order, private."

Moses grabbed the back of the sergeant's jacket and dragged him to the other side of the wall. He fell on top of the sergeant just as the predicted round landed. Ka-bloom! In a blinding flash of light, the bomb hit barrels of gunpowder stacked near the gun. A curtain of fire swept over the wall. Moses covered up as the flames raced by. His skin seemed to melt. He was being roasted alive. In a few seconds, the inferno burned out. Lifting his head, he surveyed the damage. The wall was empty. Only he and Sergeant Mac remained. The searing heat singed his hair and scorched his clothing, but Mac was saved.

Stretcher-bearers carried Mac to a makeshift hospital in one of the barracks. Wounded men spilled out of the bunks onto the floor. Above the cries of the wounded, men gossiped. The latest rumor had the fort surrendering at daybreak.

"Lad, I'll always be in your debt for saving my life, a second time," said Sergeant Mac. "But you have to save yourself. If the rumor's true, you'll have to hide out until the British leave."

"You're more important. You're in charge of the guns. I need to take care of you" Moses grumbled as he bandaged Mac's wounds. "Besides, what are they going to do, make me a slave?"

"You don't understand, lad. You're a soldier now. If they see the uniform, they'll be harder on you than the rest of us."

"Hear that," someone shouted. "It's stopped. The bombing has stopped.

"Looks like the battle is over." Mac proclaimed. "I don't know if we've won or lost, but you best be on your way before it's too late." And that's an order. If I find you here in the morning, I'll have you court-martialed."

"Aye, Aye, sir," Moses barked as he scampered out of the building. Standing outside, he wondered what he should do. He thought about ditching his uniform for some slave rags, but that was not the honorable thing to do. He was a soldier and would live and die one if necessary. Maybe, there was one more chance with Sergeant Mac.

Moses hurried to Mac's bunk and ransacked his trunk. Near the bottom, he found the bottle wrapped in a thick, brown paper. He returned to Mac's side and gently lifted the sergeant's head.

"One for the road," he said with a chuckle as he pulled the cork from the bottle of scotch whisky.

"I knew I'd make a good Scotsman out of you someday," Mac said with a raspy howl. He took a long drink and handed the bottle to Moses. "May you always walk in the Lord's shadow. Now get out of here," he said with a smile.

Moses knew there was no use in begging to stay. Mac was only looking out for him. In his heart, he knew he had to leave.

"I'll be back one day, and then you'll owe me another promotion. How does Corporal Moses sound?" Moses said, squeezing the sergeant's hand and taking a sip from the bottle. The whisky tasted horrible, even worse than the Christmas brandy. Seconds later the burning liquid revitalized his weary and aching body.

"If I have any say about it, you'll be a general," Mac joked.

Outside the air was still. In the distance, lightning cracked the sky. Daylight was still two or three hours away. There was still plenty of time to escape, but no time to waste deciding where to go. Moses tilted his head back and breathed in the cool, clean night air. Looking up, he noticed Mrs. Pickersgill's battle flag hanging limply from the pole. What he needed was a miracle. A hurricane to blow the British fleet down the bay would be perfect. Then, he could stay at the fort.

"Where can I go?" he muttered to himself as he paced the edge of the parade field. "Henry," he shouted. "No one knows the streets of Baltimore better than him."

As he headed toward the main gate, he suddenly panicked. "My drum," he screamed. "What happened to my drum?"

Moses sprinted to the top of the wall. Nothing! Everything had been swept away by the explosion. All that remained were chunks of cannon iron and a few gnarled pieces of wood.

All he could remember was placing the drum near the gunpowder while talking to Mac. Blown to bits, he figured as he searched on his hands and knees in the darkness.

"No luck. I guess I've been lucky enough tonight. I'd better leave before my luck runs out," he sighed as he stood and peered over the wall. On the ground below, he spotted a glowing, white circle. Quite odd, he thought as he leaned over for a closer look. There nestled upright in the soft earth was his drum, the drumhead reflecting the specks of moonlight. He climbed down the wall and pulled the drum from the ground. "Not a scratch on it," he noted with delight as he placed the drum in the bag.

Chapter Eleven—

Riding the Underground Railroad

Moses found the orphanage deserted. He feared the children had been evacuated. He had to find Henry. His life depended on it. Maybe, everyone was sleeping. To make sure, he tossed a couple of stones at Henry's bedroom window.

"Henry, wake up," he called out. No one appeared. He tossed a couple of more stones. Still no answer. If anyone was inside, they surely must have heard the noise. Moses had to decide his next move.

"Psst! Psst!" came the familiar sound as Henry crawled from the cellar window. "Everyone's hiding down here. What are you doing here? You're supposed to be at the fort."

"The battle is over. Sergeant Mac said I had to escape in case the British won. The fort still stands, but it's possible the city has been surrounded. Any ideas where I can go?" Moses asked anxiously.

"How about the orphanage?" Henry suggested.

"Too close to the fort," Moses replied.

"Stowaway on a ship?"

"Too far from the fort."

Henry rubbed his forehead and squinted his eyes. "I've got it," he shouted triumphantly. "The perfect place. Follow me. I'll explain as we go. There's not much time until daybreak."

Henry and Moses hiked around the south side of the harbor away from the city. After a few miles of skirting the shoreline, they rested where the main branch of the Patapsco River emptied into the harbor.

"We'll head upriver until we reach Elkridge Landing," said Henry, detailing the escape route. "We'll rest there, then head up to Ellicott Mills. I figure it's about fifteen miles."

"Then what?" Moses demanded impatiently.

"The headmaster talked about a religious group called Quakers. Calls them abolitionists because they don't believe in slavery. He also mentioned a free Negro named Benjamin Banneker. Said he was a scientist, whatever that is. Don't know if they're connected in any way, but it looks like your best chance. They might help you north."

"North?" asked an astonished Moses. "Who said anything about going north? Maybe, it's best I go back to the fort and take my chances."

"The way I see it. Heading north is your only chance for freedom," Henry replied.

"Freedom," Moses muttered under his breath. "There's that word again." As he debated what to do, the word flooded his mind. In all honesty, he really didn't have much of a choice. Back at the fort, his future was bleak. If the British won, he would be sold downriver. If the Americans won, he would be returned to the planation. Of the two choices, maybe the plantation wasn't so bad. At least, he would be with his family, but that was no guarantee. Then again, there was the problem of Hunt. He would never accept a slave as a war hero. His welcome home would be at the end of a bullwhip. Finally, the darkest of all thoughts flashed across his mind. Either way he would never see his family again. The thought had crossed his mind when he left the plantation. Now it was a fact of life.

"What are we waiting for?" Moses declared. "Let's find the road to freedom." As he took the first step, he knew he could never turn back. The words of Patayac and Frederick were proving true. The road to freedom would be a long journey with many obstacles.

They walked along the old Indian path next to the river. At daybreak, they reached the outskirts of Elkridge Landing. Through the patchy fog, they saw empty finger piers and vacant tobacco warehouses on the opposite bank. In its heyday, Elkridge Landing had been a major seaport. Ships unloaded the latest in English furniture and fashion apparel and headed downriver with hogsheads of tobacco. The gateway to the west was now a sleepy village, nothing more than a reststop for coaches running between Washington and Baltimore.

Wasting no time, Henry recited more directions. "Stay on this side of the river and keep on the path. When you come to an arching, stone bridge next to a mill, you're at Ellicott Mills. Wait until dark before going into town. Look for the Friends Meeting House. Good luck!"

Moses was stunned by Henry's hasty departure. "You're not coming along?"

"I don't think so," Henry stammered. "It's doesn't seem right."

"But if I can make it to freedom so can you. No one at the orphanage will miss you. In another year, you'll be making brooms in a factory. We're a team. Sail the widest oceans. Climb the highest mountains. Isn't that what you always said?"

Henry stared at the ground and said nothing. He was always the one to scold a hesitant Moses. Now the shoe was on the other foot. He was painfully embarrassed by his own reluctance. He had dreaded the day he would have to leave his best friend. He knew it had to come. They both had dreams of glory, yet they had to take different paths if they were to find their dreams.

"Your dream of becoming a drummer came true at the fort," Henry said. "Now your dream of freedom is somewhere far away from here. My dream of being a soldier is back at the fort. Like the day your dream came true, one day my dream will come true. That's why I must go back, and you must go ahead."

Moses nodded solemnly. He had always thought the same, but was too afraid to speak his feelings for fear of hurting Henry. "You're right, Henry. Please take this as a token of my appreciation," he said handing him the sack. "If it wasn't for you, I wouldn't have made it this far. I owe you a debt I can never repay."

Henry touched the sack and jerked his hand away. "I can't accept it. The drum is a part of you. A drummer without a drum is like a soldier without a musket. I only want your friendship." Henry said in a quivering voice. "I'll always remember you. One day when you find your freedom, you must come back to visit. You'll know where to find me. I'll be at the fort."

Moses grabbed the sleeve of his uniform jacket and ripped off the inverted stripe. He pressed the piece of cloth tightly in the palm of Henry's hand. "You'll be able to use this someday, my friend."

"Friends, forever, my brother," Henry replied sadly. He turned quickly and ran down the path, hoping that Moses did not see the tears rolling down his cheeks. That was not the way for soldiers to say good-bye.

Moses reached the mill town late that afternoon. Everything was just as Henry described. The town was nothing more than a small collection of granite buildings nestled next to the river in a steep valley. Moses took Henry's advice and hid in the woods. When the sun sank below the hills, he emerged from his lair.

The streets were deserted. The shops were closed. Merchants were home eating dinner with their families. Moses pictured the families sitting down to a big dinner with all the trimmings. His mouth watered at the thought. Some wild berries had been his only meal.

Moses walked briskly along main street. Nothing but stores lined the way. Not a church in sight. He decided to search the side streets. Luckily, there were only a few. Returning to the bridge, he followed a narrow alley. It disappeared around a sharp bend and led to the front door of the meeting house. "Perfect! Just as planned," Moses squealed. Henry was proving to be a prophet.

The doors and windows were locked. Moses waited for about an hour or so, hoping the custodian would appear. Standing in the doorway, he listened. The only sound was the constant groan from the giant mill as wheat was ground into flour. The only sign of life was a mill worker on the loading dock. When it was obvious no one was coming, he made up his mind to take his chances at the mill. It was his only chance. Fearing he might be discovered, he hid in the reeds next to the river. Finally, the miller stepped outside again. Moses approached cautiously.

"Excuse me, sir," he said politely. "I'm looking for Benjamin Banneker."

The miller paused for a moment. "Don't know anybody by that name."

"A black man who works with Mr. Ellicott."

"Doesn't sound familiar," said the man, shaking his head back and forth. "But there's some Negroes who live on the ridge. They might know."

Moses thanked the man and followed his directions. The steep dirt road led first to the Union Manufacturing Company. There a number of long and narrow brick factories housed hundreds of looms to spin cotton and wool for clothing. Beyond the complex, the road faded to a path of rutted wagon tracks which eventually led to a cluster of log cabins.

Things were going smoothly. All he had to do was find someone who could answer his questions. He stalked each cabin until he finally heard a door open. A woman, cleaning pots, stood over a bucket of water.

"Excuse me, ma'am," he called out from a distance. "I'm looking for Mr. Banneker."

The woman jumped at the sound. "Who wants to know?" she asked, turning in the direction of the voice.

"A friend looking for freedom," Moses replied.

"Well, Mr. Friend of Benjamin Banneker. I'm afraid you're late. Old Ben died about eight years ago. Ain't nothing left. His cabin burned down the day of his funeral. Him and everything he owned is nothing but ashes."

Moses was stunned by the news He was afraid this would happen. His chance for freedom was gone—up in smoke with Ben's cabin. For the first time since he left the plantation, he feared for his life. His mind raced ahead as he plotted his next move. It was too late to go back to the fort. He could just start walking, but he wasn't sure which direction to take. Now he was truly a runaway slave with a bounty on his head. He took a deep breath and sighed.

"What kind of freedom you looking for?" said the woman, sensing trouble.

"I want to go north," said Moses.

"That can be a mighty expensive trip nowadays. You better be willing to pay the price," she replied. "You best see one of them Ellicott brothers. They can help you buy a ticket. One of the brothers lives right below this hill in a big stone house. You can't miss it. You go down there and tell him Aunt Sally sent you."

Moses stumbled down the ridge. He was in a hurry. At the rate, he was going, he would know everyone in town by morning. He stopped at the first stone house overlooking the mill and knocked on the door.

"What can I do for you young man?" the woman said nervously, peering through the crack in the door. By the sound of her voice, it was obvious evening visitors were a rare occurrence.

"Miss Sally said I could find a ticket to freedom here."

"Please come in and wait. I'll call my husband."

Moses stood in the foyer and admired the fine furniture and imported rugs. The house reminded him of the Steele manor. He hoped he would receive a warmer welcome here than he ever did there. A few minutes later, Mr. Ellicott appeared in the hallway.

"Want to travel north?" he inquired, peering over the top of his bifocals resting on the top of his nose?"

"As far north as I can get," Moses replied.

"Can be arranged. Come back to the kitchen. We'll eat and talk."

Moses devoured a large bowl of stew and a plate of corn biscuits. Although exhausted from the day's journey, he eagerly recited his story about the attack on Fort McHenry. Ellicott listened attentively. He wanted to help, but there had to be no doubt to Moses' identity. It was possible that Moses could be a plant to derail the underground railroad.

"And how do I know you're telling the truth?" Ellicott asked pointedly.

"Here is my proof." Moses pulled the drum from the sack and laid it on the table. Ellicott examined the drum closely. He had been to the fort. He had seen the drummers. He was convinced.

"You'll sleep in the guest room tonight," he said, leading the way upstairs. "Only the finest for one of Baltimore's defenders."

"Are you talking about Fort McHenry?" asked Moses.

"You didn't hear?" responded a surprised Ellicott. "The word came around noon. The British sailed down the Chesapeake early this morning. Never even made it ashore."

"Good news for the fort but bad news for me," Moses said

woefully. "Now I'm a deserter and a runaway slave."

"Nonsense! You're a patriot who has earned his freedom," admonished Ellicott in a friendly tone. "Someday this country will recognize the natural rights of every man to be free."

"Does that mean I can go back to the fort?" Moses inquired.

"That could be arranged, I suppose. But there's a good chance you could be sold as a slave. You've already taken the first steps on the road to freedom. It would be a waste of time to turn back now. But it's your decision. What do you want to do?"

Moses remembered what Sergeant Mac had said before he left. He pictured his family and Luther. He remembered their dreams. He could hear them talking to him.

"Freedom at any cost," he exclaimed.

"A wise decision," Ellicott confided. "Remember, you're not running away. You're running to something better. You're doing what has to be done. Now off to bed. You've got a long journey ahead of you."

The feather mattress caressed his body like a cloud. He found Ellicott's words reassuring. Already Fort McHenry seemed like a distant memory. He found it hard to believe it was only last night he was dragging Sergeant Mac across the wall. If only Henry had come along, then everything would be right.

After a hearty breakfast of flapjacks, Moses accompanied Mr. Ellicott to the mill. Outside the office, a wagon loaded with supplies waited.

"John will be your driver for the first part of the trip," said Ellicott. "Ride with him in front of the wagon. If you're found hiding, it will only raise more questions. You'll get more information at each stop. The less you know the better." He then reached into his pocket and pulled out an envelope. "Take this," he instructed. If stopped, show this letter. It declares you're my property being shipped north to satisfy a business debt. Say no more. Have faith, Moses. I pray you'll be delivered in the hands of the Lord."

Moses thanked Ellicott for his generosity and climbed aboard. He carefully stowed his drum under the seat. The wagon slowly climbed the winding road heading west. Outside the town, the driver turned north towards Pennsylvania and freedom.

As predicted by Ellicott, the journey was long and tiresome. From sunrise to sunset, the wagon moved slowly and methodically. Its spoked wheels turned like the hands of a giant clock, counting the miles instead of the minutes. Only the changing scenery helped pass the time.

From his seat, Moses had a bird's-eye view of the countryside. For someone who had grown up on the flat coastal plain of Maryland's Eastern Shore, the landscape was breathtaking. With each passing mile, hills grew into mountains. Rivers ran fast and cold, unlike the sluggish and ebbing waterways back home. With each passing second, Moses was sure that his past was behind him, forever to be forgotten.

The routine for each day was the same. At sunset, the wagon stopped at a designated farmhouse where Moses was given a meal and a place to sleep in the attic or barn. If he was lucky, there was a hot breakfast the next morning. Before sunrise, they were on the road. Lunch was fruits and berries picked along the way. The driver did all the talking while Moses did the listening. The usual topics were farming, hunting, and the weather.

On the seventh day, the wagon passed through the town of Hope Springs, located near the northern border of Pennsylvania. Just east of the town, it reached its final destination, the small farm of Lillian and Isaac Goodwin.

"This is the last stop," said the driver. "Go on up to the porch. I see Mrs. Goodwin is waiting for you. They're real good people. I'm sure you'll do just fine with them."

The wagon departed, leaving Moses and his drum standing in the middle of the road. Moses took a few seconds to study his new home. The white clapboard house was well-kept with a fresh coat of paint. Several large oak trees shaded the lawn. At the back of the house, there was a small barn. The placed looked inviting. Moses hoped the people who lived there were just as friendly. Quite a turn of events, he thought. Who would have dreamed the road to freedom would begin on a plantation and end on a farm.

Mrs. Goodwin welcomed Moses with a hug. She was a petite woman with a warm smile. Her print dress which touched the top of her shoes made her look even smaller. Her white hair, which was tied in a bun, set her head like a halo.

"Welcome to our home, Moses," she chirped. "We've been looking forward to meeting you. I'm sure you'll enjoy your stay. Please come in and meet my husband. I'll get you something to eat. I'm sure you're tired and hungry."

Inside the parlor, Isaac sat facing the window. What he saw was a mystery to everyone since he was legally blind. However, he insisted on sitting there so he could keep an eye on the world.

"Come here, so I can see you," he said in a husky but warm voice. Isaac rose from his chair and reached forward. He caressed Moses' face and then swept his fingers along the shoulders and arms.

"Do you like what you see?" Moses asked politely. The old man's touch warmed his face like dying embers.

"I see only shadows. My hands are now my eyes."

"Then do you like what you feel?"

"I feel the presence of the Lord who has delivered a fine young man to my doorstep. You are welcome in my home as long as you wish to stay. I retired from preaching a number of years ago and now work the farm. It's only mother and myself to work the farm. The good Lord has seen fit that I outlive my children. In all truthfulness, we need help. We have a good life here, plain and simple. I hope you decide to share it with us."

After dinner, Moses sat in the parlor and recounted his life story. As usual, the drum was the center of attention. Isaac was fascinated by it. Until Lillian signaled it was time for bed, he had question after question about the drum and the plantation.

That night for the first time in his life, Moses slept in his own bedroom. No loft, no bale of hay, no horse blanket, but a mattress and pillow filled with feathers. Before closing his eyes, he thanked the god of Isaac and Olodumare for his first day of freedom. He rolled over on his side and stared at his drum on the floor. Freedom was a wonderful feeling, much like Christmas Day. Indeed, it was something to celebrate. He just hoped all of his good fortune was not a dream. He rubbed the side of his cheeks. The skin still tingled where Isaac had touched him.

The next day Moses went to the fields with Isaac. Despite his age and failing health, Isaac plowed with enthusiasm of a teenager. Moses and Isaac worked the fields until late fall, then passed the winter doing chores around the barn. Evenings were spent in the parlor, reading and talking. Lillian read and Isaac talked. Isaac loved to recall his days in the pulpit. Despite losing a son in the current war and a son and daughter to disease, he still professed an unshakable belief in his God. Certainly not odd from a man whose life and religion were one and inseparable.

Chapter Twelve—

When the Music Stopped

The winter passed without incident. With each passing day, Moses grew more comfortable with the Goodwins. By spring, he actually felt like a family member. Everyone cheered at the sight of the first robin. Milder weather was a most welcomed relief. Winters on the Eastern Shore were cold and occasionally snowy, but the winters in northern Pennsylvania were extremely harsh. Temperatures barely rose above freezing, and snowstorms made it impossible to leave the house for weeks at a time. But there was always enough love among the occupants to warm the coldest day or the coldest heart.

Even Isaac was rejuvenated by nature's rebirth. He walked stoically behind his mules and tilled the earth from memory. He talked about life, religion and farming. Frequently, he demonstrated his keen abilities to hear and smell what he could not see. In return, Moses demonstrated his abilities as a master drummer. Isaac was truly amazed that someone with the eyes of a hawk could hear like a blind man. Moses was equally amazed that a blind man could hear like a hawk.

Isaac's constant chatter had a purpose. With a lot of prodding, he eventually got Moses to open up and talk about his own life. Isaac's questions always touched on plantation religion. Moses thought it was just a passion for his life's calling. He didn't see any hidden motive. Now that spring had arrived, Isaac talked even more about religion, if that was possible. But anytime Isaac wanted to talk, Moses was willing to listen. The pupil always found the time for the wisdom of his teacher.

One Sunday after services at his church, Isaac made a peculiar request. He had Moses drive to the another church on the other side of town. When they arrived, the service was in progress.

From the outside, Moses noticed nothing unusual about the tiny church. Stepping inside, he was thunderstruck. The difference was as clear as day and night, or was it black and white. The pews were jammed with black worshipers. As he sat with Isaac in the last pew, a black preacher dressed in a scarlet robe strode to the pulpit. Reverend Maurice Kingston cleared his throat and delivered his weekly message of hope and love as only he could. Moses was spellbound. A black church with a black minister was unimaginable.

"Lord, thank you for this glorious morning. What a morning to be free," he exclaimed joyfully. "Let us sound the battle cry. Let us sing our song," he whispered softly so that heads pitched forward to catch his every word. "Let us wake up the angels of freedom. Let us wake up the devils of slavery," he clamored, his voicing slowly rising. "Let General Satan know the army of Jesus Christ will defeat his legions of slave owners. For on this glorious morning, we come to join that righteous army," he shouted passionately.

The reverend paused to wipe the sweat from his forehead. He raised his Bible high over his head with both hands. In a booming voice which shook the church to its foundation, he finished his sermon. "The Lord has spoken to me through His scripture. He said all men shall be free, regardless of their color. He freed the Israelites and one day He will free us. And believe me, brothers and sisters, it's coming soon. The judgment day for slavery is on the Lord's calendar."

"Amen, brother Maurice," came the shouts. As if on cue, the congregation rose to its feet. They held hands and sang in one glorious voice. Row upon row swayed to the music. Even Isaac who remained stone-faced throughout the sermon was now clapping and singing. Moses stood with his arms at his side rather befuddled by the whole scene. He wasn't sure what to do, so he did nothing.

After the service, Reverend Kingston greeted his flock in front of the church.

"Good to see you again, Reverend," Kingston said cheerfully, placing his hand on Isaac's shoulder.

"Always a pleasure to hear, if not see you, Reverend," replied Isaac. "I may be blind but my spirit sees your good work."

"As long as your soul sees the divine light, then I believe your sight is just fine," Kingston chuckled, patting Isaac on the back.

"You're friends with a black preacher?" Moses asked excitedly after Kingston had moved away.

"Like I said before. We are all cut from the same cloth. God's robe has many colors. But to answer your question, Reverend Kingston and I go back a number of years when his church was no more than a tent."

On the Fourth of July, Moses drove the Goodwins to town for the morning memorial service honoring the war dead. Despite the day-long festivities which also marked the end of the second war with Britain, Isaac and Lillian returned home immediately. They were eager to lay flowers on the grave of their son Jerome who was killed near the Canadian border two years ago. He was the last Goodwin offspring.

That afternoon, while Isaac and Lillian rested, Moses took his drum down to the river. He planned to observe the country's independence in his own way. After tasting his own freedom, he saw why this holiday was so important and celebrated so lavishly. Freedom, there was nothing else like it in the world.

Whenever he needed time to be alone, he always headed for the rocky bluff near Isaac's favorite fishing hole. From a ledge high above a deep pool of water, he had a sweeping view of the valley. Here he could feel the sun in his face and the wind in his hair. Here he was as free as the birds. In honor of this holiday, he drummed every march he knew. He played and sang to his heart's content. Down below, the river danced to his music and leaped at his every command. The crashing rapids roared their approval. When the concert ended, Moses sat down near the edge to simply watch the river.

"There's the drummer," someone suddenly shouted. Moses sprang to his feet to face the two young men who emerged from the woods. As they drew closer, Moses stepped forward in an attempt to hide the drum.

"Looks like we got a visitor to our swimming hole," said the taller one. "I don't think we let Negroes in our river. They might dirty up the water," he taunted as he walked over and stood inches from Moses. The boy's breath reeked from the smell of homemade liquor.

Moses stood perfectly still, waiting for them to make the first move. He had been a soldier. No doubt he could easily defend himself from these hoodlums. He slowly reached around his back for his knife. It was missing. His heart skipped a beat. With a look of frustration, he remembered he had given it to Mr. Ellicott as a token of his appreciation. Looked like he would have to simply outsmart them.

"I don't want to cause no trouble. I'll just be on my way," Moses apologized. The boys stood their ground.

"That the Goodwin's slave," said the other youth. "I've seen him in town with the old man and lady. He's working the farm with them."

"What's behind your leg?" taunted the tall one, reaching around Moses to grab the drum. In a instant, Moses lowered his shoulder and knocked away the boy's hand with his left forearm.

"Looks like we got a fight on our hands. Grab him." the boy shouted. Before Moses could react, he was knocked to his knees by a heavy blow to the stomach. As he doubled over in pain, his attacker picked up the drum and flung it into the air. Moses turned and watched in horror. The drum arched majestically through the air and splashed the water with a violent smack.

"Your turn for a bath," one of them shouted as he pushed Moses from behind.

Tumbling over the ledge, Moses heard his attackers laughing like hyenas. He looked down in horror. There was no time to panic and little time to think. The water was fast approaching. Luckily, he straightened his body and was falling head first. His only hope was to knife cleanly through the surface. Instinctively, he held out his arms to break the surface. Swaaash! Cold water exploded all around him and stung his face. His ears buzzed from the deafening splash. Cruunch! His hands snapped like kindling on the rock ledge. Stabs of blinding, burning pain shot up his arms as he slowly sank to the middle of the pool.

Holding his breath, he rolled over on his back and gazed at the sunlit surface. From this watery grave, ten feet to the surface seemed like ten miles. Time was running out. He only had a few seconds of air. He tried to swim but his hands flailed aimlessly. With his lungs ready to burst, he took his last chance. This time he stood on the sandy bottom and pushed off with his legs. The jump was just enough force to propel him upwards. Flapping his arms like a mad duck and kicking his legs like a mad stallion, he slowly rose from the depths. His head broke the surface as the last breath rushed from his body. Sucking in air, he quickly scanned the pool. No one was in sight. He would have to rescue himself.

The riverbank was only twenty yards away but Moses was drifting downriver out of control. If he didn't make it to shore, the current would surely pull him under. He didn't have the strength to free himself again. He tried to reach forward but his hands wouldn't move. His brain, wreaked with pain, stopped his body. "Be calm. All you need is a log to hang onto," he muttered to himself over and over. As he turned around, his head bumped something hard. "My drum!" he shouted as he wrapped his arms around the shell. He kicked for the shore and prayed the drum would not fill with water and sink.

Back at the house, Lillian was reading aloud Jerome's last letters when Isaac bolted to his feet.

"Something's happened to Moses," he shouted. The panic in his voice frightened Lillian. "We must hurry!"

When they stepped from the house, Isaac paced in a tight circle. "I believe he's calling from the river."

Lillian pulled him along as he gave directions. They found Moses washed up on the sand, lying on his side. They gently lifted him to his feet and dragged him home.

In the parlor, Moses curled up on the couch in agony. The pain was becoming unbearable as the numbing cold of the river wore off. Isaac gently lifted one of Moses' hands and held it in his palm. Ever so lightly, he began massaging the swollen area. Moses felt a warm, tingling sensation penetrate his skin. After a few minutes, the pain mysteriously eased. Moses closed his eyes and sighed. He wondered how Isaac had performed such a miracle.

When Lillian saw that Moses was comfortable, she prepared

a homemade remedy. Moses gulped down the bitter tasting liquid and was carried to his bed. The next morning the town doctor paid a visit and immobilized the broken hands with leather splints.

Moses was determined to get right back on his feet. It was only his hands that hurt. The rest of his body was just fine. He wasn't going to spend the whole day in bed. He had never been sick a day in his life. Despite the doctor's orders for bed rest, he knew better. On the plantation, when they laid you to rest, it was forever. He still had too much living to do before the long sleep. Besides, Isaac and Lillian needed him.

"I'm sorry to have caused you so much trouble," Moses apologized to Isaac. "You need help on the farm and I can't help. It was foolish of me to go out with the drum. People just don't understand."

"Quite all right," comforted Isaac. "My back is still strong enough to plow. Now you can be my eyes. Just don't underestimate the power of God or the determination of man. With rest and prayer, you'll be healthy in no time."

"When I'm well enough to work, perhaps it's time for me to leave," Moses suggested.

"Absolute nonsense," rebuked Isaac. Moses was surprised to see the preacher so agitated. "This land is fertile soil, the perfect place to put down roots. There comes a time and place when every man must settle down. This is definitely the place. Your time will come." He paused to let the meaning of his words sink in. "If you leave, I'll have to report you as a runaway, so I'll get you back either way," he chuckled. He walked over and put his arms around Moses.

True to his word, Moses walked the fields with Isaac. The bond between Moses and Isaac grew stronger. The normal work routine returned rather quickly. After spending all day in the fields, they rested on the porch swing before and after dinner. In the evening, Lillian read to them in the parlor.

"Perhaps you would like to read to me. You have such a fine voice," she said to Moses one evening.

"I don't know how to read," replied an embarrassed Moses. "On the plantation, it was against the law to teach a slave to read or write. You could be killed for trying."

"Well, I can right that wrong. My farm is no plantation and you're no slave. After teaching Sunday school for over thirty years, I think I'm more than qualified to teach you. Congratulations, you are now enrolled in the Goodwin College of Reading and Writing," Lillian announced with glee.

Every night Lillian spent at least an hour with her student. Although he was confused by all of the strange markings on the paper, Moses was a willing student. If reading and writing were forbidden by slave owners, then it must be good, he reasoned. For that reason alone, he was determined to read and write as well as any master. By the end of the first week, he could write his name and recite simple nursery rhymes.

Moses marveled at his success and couldn't wait for the next lesson. With each new word, his confidence soared. He wondered if his headaches weren't from all the information being crammed into his brain. Each day he looked in the mirror to see if his head had grown larger. To test his theory, he tried on the same hat every morning. Much to his disappointment, it always fit the same.

Lillian was more than glad to feed his insatiable appetite for books. Reading was changing him in ways she never imagined. Not only was Moses more comfortable around other people, but he readily voiced his opinion on a number of subjects. He and Isaac enjoyed friendly arguments over God and religion, often quoting Scripture to prove a point.

Despite all the good, Lillian was concerned. Following the attack, Moses placed his drum in the corner of his room behind a chair. He never played it again.

"Would you like me to place your drum on a table next to your bed? I can make a nice cover for it," Lillian offered.

"No. I think it's time I give the drum away," Moses replied coolly. "I've been thinking about the drum for quite awhile. Maybe I'm not meant to be a master drummer. The drum has taken me far away from home and hurt the people I love. Something is missing. Either the spirit of the drum or the spirit of the drummer has been lost."

He then grabbed a book from the table and held it above his head. "This is the future. This is the power of the universe."

That evening Moses tossed and turned in a fitful sleep. Every time he rolled on his side, he opened his eyes. Every time he found himself looking straight at his drum. Enough light came through the window to cast a dull spotlight on the black eagle. Moses stared long and hard at the figure until it appeared to move. He was afraid he was hallucinating. "You are a ghost from my past," he said sternly. "It is time to put the ghosts from the past to rest."

He could never forget the drum had brought him to freedom, but the trip was costly. Freedom was not free. That's one lesson in life he learned. "Pay the price. Pay the Price." The words of Miss Sally echoed in his mind. There was no doubt in his mind that his bill had been paid in full. The next morning he asked Lillian to take the drum from his room.

Chapter Thirteen—

In the Name of Justice

"Pull back on the reins. The plow isn't digging deep enough," Isaac instructed. Following behind the mules, he reached into the shallow furrow and grabbed a handful of dirt. Although he couldn't see the tones of the dark soil, he fingered the different textures.

"Seeds need to be buried deeper. All living things need good roots," he added wryly.

"I've been driving these horses for five years now and you're still preaching about the right way to do things," Moses laughed. By now, he knew Isaac's comments were more about living than farming.

The old preacher was always preaching. Preaching was his life. Life was what he preached. That was the way of life on Isaac's farm. It was more than a place to grow crops; it was a place to grow people.

"Never too old to learn. We stop learning; we stop living. And you're too young to do both," Isaac shot back.

With his health failing rapidly, Isaac was forced to stop working. His spirit was strong but his body weak. Now it was his turn to walk beside Moses, offering advice and providing companionship. For Isaac, the cycle of life was almost complete. As he grew older, his world became more childlike. He stood off to the side like a young boy and watched the men work. But there were no regrets. He knew his place in the grand order of the universe. Old men fall by the wayside as the young ones march by. In the autumn of his years, he was satisfied with his life. He had served God and his fellow man to the best of his ability. That in itself was enough of a reward.

While Isaac withered, Moses blossomed. He sprouted from a boy to a man, physically, mentally and spiritually. The baby-smooth complexion revealed a few wrinkles. The voice, previously nothing more than a loud whisper, was now a blaring baritone. His pencil-thin frame filled out with muscle while his brain filled with knowledge.

Reading was his passion and pleasure. Every book was a life-long friend. In the evening, he read aloud to Isaac who dozed in his chair. Books were a magic elixir to lift the spirits of both men, one tired of being sick and the other sick of being tired. Lillian made sure both men had plenty of medicine. She scoured every shop for books. The parlor walls were lined with bookcases, crammed with hundreds of books. Everyday she dusted the shelves and arranged the books in alphabetical order. Whenever she suggested that some of the books be given away, Moses rolled his eyes in mock horror.

In the fall of 1819, Isaac passed away. To the end, he was a source of inspiration. On the last day of his life, he hobbled behind the mules and clawed at the dirt. That evening, he simply laid on his bed, called Lillian and Moses to his side, and gave up his spirit. It was a dignified passing which reflected a life of dignity.

In the spring, Lillian followed. Moses saw her death coming, but was still shaken when she passed on. After Isaac's death, she simply lost her will to live. She stopped her chores and sat for hours in Isaac's chair, reading the Bible. Words of encouragement fell on deaf ears. After fifty years of marriage, she was alone and more than ready to join her family.

According to her wishes, she was buried in the family plot next to Isaac. Standing in the cold rain, Moses gazed at the pine casket and reflected on his life with the Goodwins. They were the family he had left on the plantation. They taught him how to be a man. He owed an enormous debt for the gifts they had given him. How could it possibly be repaid, he wondered. As his mind drifted, he was jolted back to reality. With Lillian gone, he was alone in the world. Her death closed the last chapter in the history of the Goodwin family. Now it was time to write a new chapter in his life, but where did he start? There were many questions to be answered. Where did he go from here? Was he a free man or a slave? He had escaped to the north, but was he really free. Once again, he was haunted by the ghosts of freedom. This time they were frightening.

After the funeral, friends of the family gathered in the farmhouse and anxiously waited for the reading of the will. Since the Goodwins had no remaining family, representatives from nearby churches arrived, hoping a portion of the estate would be left to them. Among the mourners was the Reverend William Wells, the man who succeeded Isaac as pastor of the Hope Methodist Church. The verbose and vain minister, a complete opposite of Isaac, was certain the Goodwin property would be added to the coffers of the church. Most of group agreed with his prediction.

While the crowd milled about in idle chatter, Moses stood alone at the back of the room. He knew why the mourners shunned him. He was merely part of the estate, like the mules and the horses. Then again, maybe, they considered him part of the competition for the estate. While they weren't sure why he was there, Moses knew. He was there out of respect for Lillian and Isaac, more curious than nervous. Like the others, he assumed the estate would go to Wells. It was just a matter of making it official.

Mr. Daniel Trappe, lawyer, family friend, and executor of the estate, rose to address the gathering. The winner of the Goodwin sweepstakes was about to be announced.

"Friends, on this solemn occasion, we gather to remember Lillian Goodwin and honor the last wishes of her and the late Isaac Goodwin," he announced as he broke the wax seal on the envelope. He nervously adjusted his glasses and cleared his throat. "I, Lillian Goodwin, on this day January 1, 1820, being of sound mind, upon my death, do hereby, bequeath my entire estate, to include all property and possessions, to Moses Goodwin, my adopted son in the eyes of the Almighty God, my Savior."

Chairs squeaked. Shoes scuffed the floor. People squirmed uneasily in their seats. Everyone but Trappe was shocked.

"Feeble in the mind," someone whispered.

"How can she leave everything to a Negro?" another asked. "She must have been under some kind of spell."

Hoping to silence the outburst, Trappe continued speaking.

"I, the honorable Daniel Trappe, executor of the Goodwin estate, will file this document with the county clerk tomorrow morning. In closing, let us abide by this testament and admire the generosity and compassion of Lillian Goodwin, a woman who lived her life for the greater glory of God."

"I protest this action," Reverend Wells bellowed like a bull moose. "I find it suspicious that Lillian would leave her estate to a colored boy. I do not believe Mr. Moses was officially adopted by the Goodwins. At least, I know of no records."

"The will did not state he was officially adopted, reverend," Trappe explained. "It said he was adopted in the eyes of her Almighty Savior. If you wish to take up your argument with the Lord, you, as a man of the cloth, are more qualified than me. If there is no other business, I believe my business is concluded."

"Preposterous," exclaimed an exasperated Wells. "I can attest to the fact that Reverend Goodwin, the former pastor of our congregation, stated to me on numerous occasions, even the day before he died, his estate would be given to the church. If necessary, I will contest this will to see that his last wish is granted." Wells stormed out the door in a huff.

"What does all this mean, Mr. Trappe?" asked Moses who was as stunned as anyone.

"My good man, it means the farm belongs to you. You are now a landowner in the Commonwealth of Pennsylvania. Don't worry about Wells. I can handle him. He's more interested in real estate than religion."

That evening Moses walked the fields and reflected on his good fortune. Only five years ago, the only thing he owned was the shirt on his back. Now he was a farmer with his own farm, or, at least, that's what he hoped. But Wells' threat was disturbing. What should have been a time for celebration was a time of confusion. He often heard Isaac joke about Reverend Wells and his interest in religion. It began and ended with the interest earned on the church's bank account. To Wells, God's profit line was measured in dollars not souls. If Wells protested the will, Moses was sure he would lose. He was not optimistic about retaining the farm.

True to his word, Reverend Wells filed legal papers to stop

the execution of the will. A deacon arrived at the doorstep of the county clerk an hour before opening to ensure that his suit was filed in a timely manner. After the suit was logged, Wells held a press conference on the courthouse steps. Tearfully, he told the audience that he had committed his life to ensure that Isaac's last wish was honored. To pursue that noble commitment, he had secured the legal services of Mr. Bradford Sterling, a high-powered lawyer from the prestigious Philadelphia law firm of Cockburn, Ross and Sterling. Victory was guaranteed.

When Moses heard the bad news, he began packing his belongings. He hoped to get out of town before anyone could question his status as a free man. It was time to head north once again. He was a well-seasoned traveler. He knew how to survive on the road. Maybe one of these years, he would reach the land of his ancestors wherever it may be. Only the last-minute pleas of Trappe convinced him to stay and see it to the end. Trappe was right. He owed that much to the Goodwins.

When the travelling judge arrived two weeks later, courtroom fever peaked. People crowded the streets as if it was the Fourth of July. Hope Springs had been whipped into a frenzy from the pulpit of Reverend Wells who every Sunday anointed himself as the messenger of God. With help from the Almighty, he vowed to overcome this great miscarriage of justice.

The town mayor, seizing the opportunity to win votes in the next election, declared the day a holiday. Every man, woman and child wanted a courtroom ticket. They were convinced this decision would be a legal landmark in American history. In reality, the hearing never made it beyond the local newspapers. But it was a major scoop for local reporters. On the street corners, bets were wagered to see which barrister would prevail. The odds-on favorite was Mr. Sterling, the dapper, city dandy who let it be known to anyone within earshot that no country bumpkin could defeat him in a court of law.

A hush fell over the crowd when the Reverend Wells and his rotund lawyer entered the courtroom. Sterling strode confidently to his table. He certainly walked to the beat of a different drummer, tapping his customized cane with every other step and puffing on an enormous, and no doubt expensive, cigar like a steam engine.

"Sterling as in sterling silver. As good as money in the bank," he introduced himself to the gallery. Once seated, he leaned back in his chair and blew smoke rings at the spectators. His briefcase remained closed. He was on record as saying the hardest part of this trial would be finding a first-class restaurant for the victory banquet.

Across the aisle, Trappe poured over last-minute notes and conferred with Moses. He wanted to ensure Sterling wouldn't be able to spring any surprises. In his mind, he had an airtight case.

The judge cleared his throat and called the court to order. The rules of the hearing were quickly established. Both lawyers agreed the judge's ruling would be final. There would be no appeals. This contest was winner take all; loser take the fall. Mr. Sterling was first to address the court. He walked to the front of the judge's bench and turned to face the crowd.

"Your honor, I petition the court to void the will of Mrs. Lillian Goodwin for any of the following reasons. First, Mrs. Goodwin was not mentally capable of making a sound decision due to her depression over her husband's death. Second, the Reverend Isaac Goodwin desired that his estate be given to the Hope Methodist Church. And third, Mr. Moses has no legal claim to the Goodwin estate. We know Lillian Goodwin was a good Christian woman who wanted to perform a deed of charity by leaving her estate to this Negro boy, but the wishes of her husband must prevail as head of the family."

After some lengthy blabbing about the holy intentions of Reverend Wells, Sterling finally relinquished the floor. Mr. Trappe stood in place and read his opening remarks. The paper jumped nervously in his hands. With his rumpled suit and thick glasses, he looked more like a bookkeeper than a lawyer. His appearance and opening remarks did not impress Moses. After seeing Trappe's performance, he had reason to worry. Trappe was quickly letting the air out of an airtight case.

"Your honor, I contend the document executed and signed by Mrs. Goodwin is legal and binding," Trappe droned. "Until Mr. Sterling can produce a document signed by Mrs. Goodwin stating otherwise, the court has no option but to dismiss the petition of Reverend Wells and certify that Mr. Moses is the rightful heir to the Goodwin estate."

Next it was Sterling's turn to attack. Sterling, the consummate showman and ringmaster, took control and turned the proceeding into a spectacle. Throughout the morning, he led an endless parade of witnesses who swore to Lillian's state of melancholy after Isaac's death. Trappe had to reluctantly agree that Lillian was somewhat distraught over the death, but argued it in no way impaired her thinking. In the afternoon, Sterling followed the same route. This time the procession of witnesses swore on a stack of Bibles they heard Isaac Goodwin declare his intent to leave his estate to the church.

Before each witness, Trappe objected to the hearsay evidence. Each time he was overruled. The witnesses were allowed to testify. After each witness, Trappe asked for documentation to verify any of their claims. Each time, there was none. Finally, Wells ran out of witnesses, the day ran out of time, and the judge ran out of patience. Shadows of late afternoon streaked across the floor. The judge squirmed in his chair, shuffled some papers, and asked both lawyers to stand. He had heard enough. And now the winner of the Goodwin estate was to be officially sanctioned by the State of Pennsylvania. Everyone held their breath.

"Gentlemen, I have listened to the testimony and read the documents pertaining to this case. In my opinion, Mrs. Goodwin was depressed over the death of her husband, but there is no medical evidence to question her state of mind. Likewise, there are no documents from Mr. Goodwin that bequeath his estate to the church. Mr. Sterling, if you have no further evidence, I must rule in favor of Mr. Moses. In his possession, he has a legal and binding document."

"Your honor, there is one more fact," said Sterling with a sinister grin. "I respectfully ask the court to consider the status of Mr. Moses. As a runaway slave, he is not a citizen of this state, and, therefore, does not enjoy the privileges accorded to its legal residents. He has no right to own, transfer or receive property." Sterling stood triumphantly. He folded his arms across his chest and stared hard at Trappe. Picking up his cigar, he turned and winked at the crowd.

"What brilliance! What timing!" came the cries from the gallery. They applauded and honored this legal legend with a standing ovation. Money was ready to change hands. The slick, city lawyer waited until the last hand to play his trump card.

Trappe was stunned. He turned to Moses and shrugged his shoulders. The only thing he could do was hope to buy time.

"Your honor, in light of this last statement, I respectfully ask the court to recess until tomorrow morning. I'm certain Mr. Sterling would agree that I need time to determine the legal status of my client."

Sterling agreed. Victory was great, but a chance to slowly humiliate your opponent was even better. Another day of adulation from these country bumpkins suited him fine.

The judge nodded his head in approval. "The court will recess until 9 o'clock tomorrow morning. At that time, the case will proceed without delay."

After the courtroom emptied, Trappe sat down with Moses and explained their options. In reality, he was stating their chances of winning; slim and none.

"We lost. Just like that," Moses said, snapping his fingers. "I should have known a Negro would never get justice. No matter where, north, south, east or west." He really couldn't blame Trappe. Trappe gave it his best shot. The cards were stacked against him and he knew it. Wells was dealing from the bottom of the deck and no one cared.

"It's legal. That's all that matters," Trappe replied dejectedly. "In this business, you learn quickly that truth and justice are not always the same. I'm going home to study my law books. Maybe, I'll find a loophole. There's always a chance to win. We just have to find it before tomorrow. Improbable but not impossible."

"Mr. Trappe, I have yet to find someone who found a needle in the haystack, but you're more than welcome to look," said a disappointed Moses. He headed home with a tormented look upon his face. Losing the estate wasn't the worst thing that could happen. Sterling was questioning his legal status. Losing his freedom was a distinct possibility. But despite all the worry, he wasn't going to run. He would make his last stand in Hope Springs.

Moses stood in the parlor and cried out in the darkness. "Isaac! Lillian! I've come too far to be abandoned. This is my home! Help me keep it." He slumped in Isaac's chair and sighed. There must be something someone can do, but who and what? They were questions with no answers.

"Moses! I think I've got it," Trappe shouted, bursting through the front door like an raging bull. "If we can somehow prove you're a legal slave but not a runaway slave then we can claim you have a right to the property."

"If I say I'm any kind of slave, someone will kidnap me and sell me down south. I'm as free as I need to be. No one owns me anymore," Moses declared passionately.

"But are you really free?" Trappe replied tersely. Moses looked into Trappe's eyes and lowered his head. He knew what the lawyer meant. He would never be free until he stood up for what he believed. After the plantation and Fort McHenry, how far would he have to go to find freedom?

"Let me get this straight. You want me to say I'm a slave?"

"Not just say it, prove it," advised Trappe. "You have to prove that you were the property of the Goodwin's and not a runaway. Then, we can make a legal claim."

"That's impossible. Everyone knows they hated slavery. It would be dragging their names through the mud. I could never forgive myself if I did that."

"Moses, those two old people loved you like their own son," scolded Trappe, grabbing Moses by the shoulders. "They wanted you to have this land. That's all they ever talked about to me. I promised them I would see it done. And besides, that's our only chance."

When Trappe left, Moses slumped back in the chair. Trappe had a great plan, but that's all it was. He needed proof not promises.

"Nothing ventured, nothing gained," Moses mumbled to himself. Any thing of value belonging to Isaac and Lillian was in their bedroom. That was the only place to search. There wasn't much to find. In the dresser, there was a small box filled with letters, birth certificates, marriage licenses and diplomas. Everything to document the history of the Goodwin family, but nothing in the way of business records. Moses returned to the parlor, satisfied that he had done all he could. It was now up to Trappe to turn the tables of Sterling and spring a surprise. He hoped Trappe could live up to his name and ensnare his opponent.

Moses accepted his fate with sad resignation. What he needed was a good book to soothe his troubled soul. Scripture always comforted Isaac, perhaps, it could do the same for him. Although he read every book in the house, he had never picked up the family Bible. As he reached for the thick and heavy book on the edge of the table, it slipped from his fingers and fell to the floor. Silk bookmarks spilled out.

Picking up the book, Moses noticed a letter protruding from the bottom. Not unusual because Isaac used Jerome's letters as bookmarks for his favorite passages. He was ready to simply push the letter back into its place when his curiosity got the best of him. He had never read any of the letters. Maybe there, he would find the peace that Isaac always found. He carefully unfolded the brittle, yellow document and began to read.

Holding the letter high above his head, he fell to his knees. "Thank you Isaac! Thank you Lillian!" he shouted in ecstasy. The Book of Exodus, Chapter 33, held the answer to his prayers. The impossible was now the unbelievable. Truly a miracle, Moses thought. Tomorrow, he would find out if Reverend Wells and Mr. Sterling believed in supernatural powers. He folded up the paper and hurried to Trappe's home.

The next morning in court Mr. Trappe delivered his closing argument with a poise and confidence never seen. "Your honor, I believe we can put this matter to rest. I would like to sincerely thank my colleague, Mr. Sterling. Due to his suggestion, I can finally verify and authenticate the last will and testament of Lillian Goodwin."

"Please proceed," the judge said dryly. "But remember, the law is quite clear on the rights of citizens and slaves."

Sterling gloated at his table with a grin from ear to ear. He rolled his unlit cigar from one corner of his mouth to the other. This was going to be better than he thought. The last attempt by Trappe would be great theater, a tragic comedy to be enjoyed by all.

"Your honor, I would like to submit this shipping receipt as legal proof that Mr. Moses was not a runaway slave but the legal property of the Goodwins. Therefore, as part of the estate, Mr. Moses retains rights to control the estate. In essence, Mr. Moses has inherited himself and is now legal guardian and rightful heir to the Goodwin estate."

The gallery hooted and hollered. The hometown hero had prevailed. David slew Goliath; Trappe slew Sterling. "What brilliance! What timing!" they shouted. "Can't outsmart an old country boy," they hollered. They knew Trappe would win all along.

Sterling's cheeks turned crimson and filled with air like a giant balloon. His eyes bulged from their sockets as he bit down hard on his cigar. Any second his head would explode. A gurgling sound in his throat ignited the cranial dynamite. "Pa-too-ey!" The enormous cigar rocketed across the room and crashed into the wall behind the judge. Wells launched from his chair, knocked over his table, and raced to the bench.

Peering over the judge's shoulder with the look of a wild man, he constantly blinked his eyes. He couldn't believe what he was seeing. This couldn't be happening. The judge held the paper at arm's length and began to read. "The possessor of this bill is the legal owner of the attached property, one male slave of African descent, approximately 14 years of age, called by the Christian name of Moses. I certify this property, free of any taxes or liens, is being transferred to the holder as payment for a business debt which releases the undersigned from any further financial responsibility. Given freely by me, John Ellicott, president of the Ellicott Mills Company, this day September 15th in the Year of our Lord 1815."

Underneath the signature and seal of John Ellicott were the signatures of Isaac and Lillian Goodwin, dated September 21, 1815."

The gallery erupted in thunderous applause.

"Order in the court," the judge pleaded. "In light of this evidence, the court rules the will of Lillian Goodwin to be legal and binding. For the record, all documents pertaining to this case will be registered with the county clerk and entered in the state archives."

"I protest this action," Sterling shouted in a futile attempt to sway the judge. "Your honor, since the court has decided that Mr. Moses is legally a slave, I petition the court that as property of the

Goodwin estate, he be transferred to my client."

Sensing that Sterling was about to pull a rabbit out of his hat, Trappe slowly rose to his feet. The gallery fell silent. He had anticipated Sterling's next move and was prepared to deliver a knock-out punch.

"Your honor, due to the fact that Mr. Moses is a landowner in the State of Pennsylvania by your decree, and now enjoys all the rights and privileges thereof, let a public notice be posted on this day that Mr. Moses has granted himself freedom from the bonds of slavery and declared himself a citizen. I have prepared all documents for your signature. My client humbly asks the court to record a name change. From this day forward, Mr. Moses will be legally recognized as Moses Freeman."

"Objection! Objection, your honor," Sterling screamed. He pounded his cane on the floor until it snapped like a dead twig.

"Mr. Sterling, your objection is overruled. Mr. Trappe, your requests are granted," the judge replied. "Gentlemen, this case is closed."

Sterling scooped up his papers and stormed from the courtroom with Reverend Wells on his heels. Victory dinner would be a heaping pile of fresh crow. Moses and Trappe danced a jig as well-wishers showered them in confetti.

"We did it Moses. We beat the odds and the best lawyer money could buy," Trappe shouted with glee.

"Not exactly, Mr. Trappe," Moses said with a chuckle. "I think we had some help from Isaac and Lillian. And what's this name change all about?"

"Sorry, Moses, but I needed a last name for the documents, and I didn't have time to check with you. I thought Freeman was the perfect choice so I took the liberty."

"Freeman. Free man," Moses repeated several times, rolling the words over his tongue. "I like it a lot. It has a nice ring to it."

"If my services are no longer needed, I'll be on my way," said Trappe merrily. "Just remember, all's well that ends Wells."

The courtroom quickly emptied. Most of the crowd raced behind Sterling and Wells. They were holding a press conference in the street, denouncing the grave injustice of the court. Moses, hoping to avoid the spotlight, tried to sneak out the back door.

"Congratulations, Mr. Moses Freeman," said Reverend Kingston with a wide smile and a firm handshake. "Looks like you lost your seat in Reverend Wells' church today. But don't worry, there's more than one church around here. Maybe you can visit us on Sunday. It's the same God just a different home. We'd be glad to see you."

"Thanks for the offer, Reverend. I think it's time I found a spiritual home. I think Isaac would like that."

Moses was overwhelmed by the court's decision. All the way home he cried tears of joy. Not only was he a certified landowner but officially a free man. His wildest dream had come true, and he owed it all to Isaac and Lillian. Right then and there, he vowed to follow in their footsteps. While he couldn't be a man of the cloth, he could certainly become more familiar with the fabric.

The evening was not a time for celebration but for commemoration. Moses placed a bouquet of flowers on the graves of Isaac and Lillian and read eloquently from the Book of Exodus. The warm breeze carried his words to the heavens like the wings of an eagle.

"The Lord told Moses and the people whom have been brought up from the land of Egypt to go up from here to the land which I swore to Abraham, Isaac and Jacob I would give to their descendants."

That Sunday after services, Reverend Kingston stood at the back of the church and engaged his flock.

"Good morning, Moses," he said cheerfully. "It's a fine morning to be saved. I'm delighted you accepted my offer." As the reverend spoke, Moses gazed at a group of young people standing on the lawn. Seeing that his new parishioner was distracted, the reverend stood on his toes to see what was interfering with the work of the Lord. "For heaven's sake," he intoned in a voice loud enough to attract Moses' attention.

"Oh, sorry Reverend," Moses apologized. "I seem to be gazing while your flock is grazing," he laughed.

"The Lord and the ladies," responded Kingston with a chuckle of his own. "Now I see God's plan and yours quite clearly. My, my, the Lord works in strange ways. You wait right here while I gather my sheep."

A few minutes later the reverend returned. "Miss Thomas. I'd like you to meet Mr. Moses Freeman who just recently joined our church."

"Oh, that's the absolute truth, ma'am. With the Reverend's help, I have found the spirit to save my lonely soul," Moses said with a widening smile. He didn't dare say the spirit he had in mind was standing in front of him.

The young lady curtsied and took her cue with a nod from the Reverend. "Reverend Kingston has talked so highly about you. It's such a pleasure to meet you. Please call me Harriet," she said with a delicate voice like that of an angel.

The next Sunday Moses was the first one in church, hoping to catch a glimpse of the lovely Miss Harriet. If he was really lucky, he hoped to sit near her. All week in the fields, he rehearsed what he would say if he had the chance to speak to her. He hoped his chance was today. As luck would have it, Harriet sat on the other side of the aisle. Out of sight but not out of mind.

After the service ended, Harriet stood in the foyer, obviously waiting for someone. How I wish it was me, Moses thought as he headed for the door. Slowly he walked passed her, too afraid to even glance in her direction.

"Moses, I've been waiting to see you," Harriet called. "My sister is having a picnic next Saturday at her farm. I was wondering if you would like to be my date."

"Ah, well! Ah, yes! Of course! It would be my pleasure," Moses said fumbling with his words. Despite all of his rehearsing, he panicked. He blew his lines like an amateur actor on opening night. After Harriet gave him the directions, he hopped aboard the wagon with an extra spring to his step. "I must be dreaming," he said to himself over and over again. For good measure, he pinched himself on the arm.

Chapter Fourteen—

Return of the Night Walker

Harriet lived on the Walker farm with her sister Millie. It was a two-hour ride north of Hope Springs from the Goodwin place. Moses snapped hard on the reins, anxious to start. The horses responded by breaking into a brisk trot. Moses was excited about seeing Harriet but petrified about meeting the rest of her family. Other than Harriet and Reverend Kingston, the guests would be unnamed faces from church. When the wagon finally turned down the lane, Harriet came running from the house.

"Hurry up, Moses," she called. "I've been waiting for you all morning. Don't you worry about the wagon. Hand those reins to the boys. That's their job if they want apple pie."

As Moses climbed down, Harriet kissed him on the cheek. "You'll have a wonderful time. Don't be nervous. Come on around back. I'll introduce you to everyone." For Moses, the day was off to a great start.

They walked to the back of the house where a smattering of elders and children sat in the shade. The women prepared the food while the men congregated near a small barrel which, no doubt, held a strong cider. Every few seconds, one of the men glanced over his shoulder to ensure that Reverend Kingston was not ready to preach about the spirits, especially the distilled variety. To Moses, the scene was reminiscent of the Christmas frolics on the plantation. Only the plantation never had such gatherings in the middle of the summer.

"So this is home?" Moses asked in an awkward attempt to start a conversation.

"Until I settle down on a place of my own. But first, I have to find the right man to settle down with," Harriet replied, squeezing Moses by the arm. "I mainly tend to my sister's four children while she and her husband work the farm."

"Well, there you are," Millie called out from the kitchen. "Now come over here and introduce me to this handsome gentleman." Moses swallowed hard at Millie's comment.

"This is Moses Freeman, the young man from church," Harriet said. "Isn't he cute?"

"A pleasure to meet you Moses," Millie replied. Moses blushed. The likeness of the sisters was striking. They had the same delicate features and soft voices. The differences were minor. Millie was four years older and slightly taller.

"I want you to meet my husband, but he's always in the fields. Even on the day of the picnic, he has chores. Sometimes, he stands out there in the dirt like he's taking root. I've never seen a man more at peace walking behind a plow. Perhaps, you would be so kind as to go and fetch that man," she said to Moses apologetically. "Tell him the food is on the table. He's over in the corner of that field," she said, pointing with a finger to a distant tree line.

"My pleasure. I know what it's like to walk the fields," replied Moses, eager to escape the girl talk for a few minutes.

Moses walked toward the trees. His shoes sunk in the thick, black earth which had been soaked by the recent rains. With each step, the silhouettes of a man and a horse loomed larger. Millie's husband can't be bad if he enjoys his farm, he thought.

As he drew closer, he looked down at the fresh footsteps. Stopping dead in his tracks, he bent down and traced each foot print with his finger. One foot left a unique, yet familiar print. "Impossible," Moses uttered as he started to walk again. It was obvious this farmer not only worked in his bare feet but suffered some kind of deformity.

When he was about a hundred yards from the man, Moses stopped again. He remembered when he had seen the footprint. Cupping his hands to his mouth he called out. "Katumbe Katumba! Katumbe Katumba!

The man in the field dropped his hands from the plow, shaded his eyes with his hand, and moved forward. "My God! I don't believe it. It's Moses!" he shrieked. He ran so fast across the furrows that he tripped and fell not once but twice. Each time he picked himself up and ran faster.

The two men raced into each other's arms. After a long embrace, they stood back and stared in disbelief.

"You're alive," squealed Moses with joy. "You're supposed to be dead. Drowned in the bay."

"You're free," shouted Luther with a wide grin. "You're supposed to be a slave on the plantation."

The two men walked side by side to the farmhouse. With every step, they went farther back in time. They talked hurriedly as if they only had a few minutes together, often interrupting each other questions.

"I forgot to tell you," said Moses. "Your wife said it's time to eat."

"With that woman, it's always time for me to do something," Luther joked.

Moses raced a few steps ahead and turned to Luther. "I'll always be my own man. I'll never take orders from anyone. I'll never be a slave to any man," he taunted playfully. "Did that statement also include any woman?"

Luther laughed at the sound of his own words. "That's right, house boy," he replied. "I said any man, not any woman."

"You married?" Luther asked.

"No," replied Moses. "At least not yet, but I've got my eye on a pretty filly."

"You know my wife Millie has a sister that just might be looking for a husband."

"Yeah, I know," said Moses. "She invited me to the picnic."

"You mean to tell me Harriet's been blabbing all week about Mr. Steele's stable boy. You'd better watch yourself with her. She's a fine woman, but just as stubborn and independent as her sister. They're dangerous," he chuckled. "They not only talk about freedom for the Negroes. They talk about freedom for women. In my book, they're way ahead of their time, but I don't dare say anything. My, oh my, how the world is changing."

Moses and Luther talked until the early morning. Harriet and Millie sat by their sides and listened to the boyhood tales of adventure. Millie was glad to have finally discovered the hidden side of her husband. Luther rarely talked about his days as a slave. He often acted as if he was ashamed of the fact. Tonight was different. Tonight he was face to face with his past and enjoying every minute of it. Millie knew he had the right to be proud of his past life as well as his present.

"That raft was just a decoy. I threw some clothes on it and cut it free from my canoe. When the storm hit, I lashed myself to the canoe. The last thing I remembered was being crushed by a giant wave. The next morning, I awoke on the beach still tied to the canoe. When I saw the sun rising at my back, I knew I made it across the bay. Then I just started walking north. Two months later, I was in Pennsylvania. With the help of Reverend King, I was settled on the Walker farm. Worked hard. Saved my money. Before I knew it, I had a farm and a family."

Moses told his story from the attack on St. Michael's to the Battle of Baltimore. He detailed his life with the Goodwins and noted with pride that he could read and write. Never once did he mention the drum.

"Is freedom as good as I said it would be?" Luther asked sincerely.

"I'm afraid you were wrong. It's not at all like you described. It's better," Moses kidded. "So now that you have your freedom, what is your dream?"

Luther grimaced. It was the same question he posed to Moses years ago. Now he knew how tough it was to answer. "My dream is here on this farm with Millie. My dream is that one day my children will grow up and be able to live and work anywhere in this great land."

"And what about your dream of becoming a regimental drummer?" he asked.

Moses paused. It had been years since he had thought about the drum. "I guess my dream about being a drummer was all about my dream of freedom. It was the drum that brought me this far. But that's part of the past. It's time for new dreams." He intentionally left the question unanswered.

On the ride home, Moses remembered his life on the plantation. They were bittersweet memories, times of innocent happiness and unimaginable horror. He was glad to see Luther had found a place to put down roots. If anything, he was jealous that Luther lived his dream and accepted the fact that he would never see his home or family again. Moses was still tormented. Time had not healed all of his wounds. In the back of his mind, the question of his own family haunted him. How can I live my own dream of freedom when my family lives in slavery, he constantly debated. The thought weighed him down like a stone tied around his neck.

Back at the house, he was too excited to sleep. Images of Luther and Harriet danced in his head to the music of his soul. It was a strange but familiar rhythm. It was the same one he heard many years ago.

As the music slowed and he drifted off to sleep, he thought about his drum. He wondered what Lillian had done with it. Most likely, it ended up as kindling on a cold winter day. Or at least, that's what he hoped. According to Frederick, a consecrated drum must be offered to the gods on a flaming altar. This was normally done after the death of its owner, the master drummer. I'm still alive, Moses reckoned. So there was no need to really worry. And besides, that part of his life was behind him. History was for the dead, not the living, he reasoned.

The next morning Moses searched his book collection. He looked for the ones Lillian had used to teach him to read. His offer to teach Luther was sheer genius. Now he had a weekly invite to the Walker farm. Luther would be a formidable challenge, but the rewards were great. The quicker Luther learned to read, the more time he had to spend with Harriet. To Moses, it was more than a fair bargain. No, to be more exact, it was a downright steal. He couldn't wait to begin.

Moses and Harriet quickly became constant companions. In the interest of Luther's education, Moses traveled to the Walker farm at least twice a week. After class, he and Harriet walked down to the stream and held hands. Their hearts blossomed like the wild flowers which edged the path. No longer did Moses have to corner Harriet to steal a kiss. She gave herself freely. In his arms, her tender body trembled like that of a captive sparrow.

By fall, Moses was ready to replace his summer love with something more permanent. On that fateful evening, he snuggled next to Harriet on their customary stroll. The night was unseasonably cold with a bite of winter in the air. Leaves flitted to the ground like snowflakes. In the fading sunset, trees radiated brilliant hues of brown, gold and red. The perfect setting, Moses thought as he tried to remain calm. By the time they reached the stream, his stomach was churning like a volcano. He had rehearsed this scene again and again. Now that the moment had finally arrived, he felt the words sliding down his throat. It was just like the first time he met her.

Standing on the stream bank, his heart fluttered and his knees buckled. On this evening, Harriet had never looked more beautiful. As she looked away, the moon cast a soft hue on her face. Moses took her hand and pulled her to his chest.

"Will you marry me?" he blurted out with a sigh of relief.

"Yes, my love," Harriet whispered softly, gently kissing Moses along the neck and cheek until their lips met in a sweet, passionate embrace. Moses tingled with goose bumps as her breath warmed his skin. The exotic fragrance of her perfume was intoxicating. His senses were overwhelmed. Pressing his body next to hers, he felt their hearts beat as one. For the very first time, their souls touched. For hours, they sat huddled in each other's arms. They gazed into each other's eyes and saw a future as bright as the stars in the sky. It was an enchanted evening where lovers dream, and no dream seems impossible. Time not only stopped, but the clock of the universe was reset to mark the beginning of a new life together.

"Harriet! Harriet!" Millie called out in the night, breaking the magical spell.

"We're over here," Harriet replied.

"You two turtle doves best fly back to the nest before the morning's first light. You mean to tell me you've been out here all night looking at the stars." Millie smiled as the love birds headed back to the house. She fondly remembered the days when Luther came courting. They had walked the same path and spent hours snuggled together, gazing at the stars.

Moses and Harriet were married on the first Saturday in November. That afternoon, Harriet wore Millie's gown, and Moses borrowed Luther's suit. Reverend Kingston stood like a doting father and pronounced the couple husband and wife. Moses slipped a thin gold ban around Harriet's finger. The ring was a special symbol of love. Lillian had given it to him with the promise that he give it to his bride on his wedding day. Following a short reception at the church, the newlyweds returned home. Moses carried Harriet across the threshold and deposited her in the parlor. He disappeared into the kitchen and returned with a broom.

"Let this broom sweep away the bitter history of those who have gone before us. Let this break the last link in my chains of slavery," Moses said solemnly.

"You know how I feel about those African ways of yours, Mr. Moses Freeman," Harriet said, feigning anger and shaking her finger at Moses. "Let this be a symbol of our new life together as a free man and woman."

Moses threw the broom on the floor and grabbed Harriet's hand. Laughing aloud, they jumped over the broom as husband and wife. Moses then picked Harriet up in his arms, literally sweeping Harriet off her feet.

Chapter Fifteen

The Homecoming

The marriage prospered. In a short time more than crops were springing up on the Goodwin spread. A year after the wedding, their first daughter Henrietta was born. She was followed by Francine in 1825 and Margaret in 1828. Finally, in 1830, the first male of the Freeman family was born into freedom and baptized with the Christian name of Henry. With an heir to the family name and hopefully the family tradition, Moses considered his life complete. But the feeling of contentment was short-lived. Shortly after Henry's first birthday, Moses began having his dream. At first, it was once a month, then once a week. He was worried. Was this some kind of omen or was he losing his sanity, he wondered.

The dream was always the same. He stood on a ledge high above a raging river. Dark gray clouds raced overhead in a continuous circle and unleashed a cold, hard rain. On the distant horizon, a hazy sun pulsated with a fading reddish-orange light like a giant heart. Directly across from him on the opposite ledge perched a black eagle. Only this eagle was as tall as a man. Moses called out, but the howling wind made it impossible to hear. Each cliff dweller stood his ground. The eagle's eyes burned with rage. Moses stared hard. Neither blinked.

In the fiery glow of the eagle's gaze, Moses saw his own reflection. It was a shocking and terrifying sight, a monstrous figure that only a dream could produce. Moses had become half-man and half-eagle. His arms were feathered wings and his feet were razor-sharp talons. As he studied his bizarre image, the eagle flapped its wings and took flight. When the clouds momentarily parted, the great bird raced for the opening. Each time, it was knocked from the sky with a fierce flash of lightning. Once, twice, it faltered from the vicious blow of an invisible fist. On the third attempt, the eagle was hurled into the river with a thunderous splash.

The eagle went under and never reappeared. Bobbing to the surface were the heads of his father, mother and sister. They frantically waved their arms for help. Moses dove from the ledge. Just before he splashed the water, his family disappeared under the waves. The dream ended. As always, Moses bolted upright, his nightclothes drenched in sweat and his heart pounding wildly.

The dream was not the only unusual occurrence. The night of the dream always followed a day of eerie silence in the fields. On these days, the air was still. Not a bird or beast stirred. Even the flocks which scavenged the freshly plowed earth were missing. Moses was cut off from the living world. His ears had gone deaf. It was as if the farm had been deserted, or worse yet, as if the farm had died.

After days of soul searching, Moses concluded these were supernatural signs. That was the only explanation. Since leaving the plantation, he always harbored the thought of his family. Now for some unexplained reason, the thought had been unleashed in his mind by a mysterious force. The dream called him for a purpose. It would not end until that purpose had been fulfilled.

"Hattie, I must go back and rescue my family," Moses said one morning at breakfast. "Long ago when I was a young boy, I dreamed of the black eagle. Now the eagle has come back for me."

Harriet listened intently. She was relieved that Moses had decided to talk. "I've watched you night after night. I knew you were troubled, but I knew you had to work it out on your own." She searched for the words to let Moses know that she supported him. "You're as stubborn and bullheaded as me. But you must do what your heart tells you. If your heart tells you to go, then by all means go. But make sure you have a plan. You could be killed or, even worse, captured. Your freedom is at stake."

"I know, my dear," replied Moses. "But I will never be free as long as my family is enslaved. I must go back and find them."

Harriet held Moses in her arms and laid her head on his chest. "You have my blessing," Harriet whispered. "Take my love with you. It will comfort you in your time of need."

For the rest of the week, Moses pondered his decision. Harriet was right about the dangers. He was risking his freedom. Even after all of these years as a free man, he could be returned to the plantation as a runaway. The bounty on his head remained for the rest of his life and increased yearly. By now, he was worth a small fortune, dead or alive.

That Saturday on his weekly trip into town, he found his answer. Next to the general store, he glanced at an Indian family huddled in the alley. For some reason, he did a double take as he turned the corner. There was nothing special to see, yet he was compelled to look. He witnessed this scene many times, another homeless family from a homeless tribe heading West after being run off their land. He knew the feeling of being abandoned. It always left a knot in his stomach. Of all people, he was the one who should help, but for some reason, he always felt powerless.

Today was going to be different, Moses vowed. He would help in some small way, maybe food, clothing or money. When he jumped from the wagon and walked down the alley, the family was gone. They had disappeared into thin air. He searched behind the buildings. Not a soul in sight. Returning to where the family was sitting, he found a black and white feather on the ground. A gentle smile spread across his face. He remembered where he had seen one of the family members. The old man bore a remarkable resemblance to Patayac. "How strange!" he muttered. "After all of these years, the old Indian has returned." He tossed the feather in the air. It floated to the heavens. A good omen, he thought. He was sure he had made the right decision.

Sunday after church, Moses cornered Luther and talked to him about his plan. He knew Luther sheltered runaway slaves at his farm. If anyone could help, it was Luther. He had the contacts in the region.

"I'll need an escort through Maryland and passage across the bay," Moses explained.

Luther nodded his head in agreement. "I think the arrangements can be made. I'll have an answer on Sunday."

The following Sunday Luther gave Moses the good and bad news. "I can get you across the bay, but you have to travel to the plantation by yourself. I'm dealing with new people from another state. They feel it's too dangerous to liberate the plantation. It would be a messy political situation if they were captured with you."

"If that's the best you can do, then it's a risk I'm willing to take," replied Moses. "When do I leave?"

"Two weeks from now, Sunday after next. That will give me time to make the final arrangements."

On the second Sunday, Moses said good-bye to his family and rode to the Walker farm. When he arrived at the barn, Luther and another man were standing by their horses.

"Andrew will be your guide. He'll take you to the bay and bring you back. Listen to what he says. He's the best in the business," said Luther. "And one more thing. Since this mission is too risky for the others, I've decided to go along."

Moses was surprised at Luther's comment. In two weeks of planning, Luther was never mentioned. "I'm sorry, Luther, but you can't go. Someone has to look after the families. You've already paid a steep price for your freedom. I can't ask you to pay any more. Maybe another time, but not now."

"I understand," said Luther with a frown. "But remember, freedom has no final price tag. It's something we pay for everyday of our lives. Now go with peace of mind. I'll take care of everything."

Moses and Andrew rode into the night, stopping only to eat and rest. Andrew was a broad, big-boned young man who looked much older than his age. His weathered face and calloused hands reflected many hard years behind a plow in some barren field. With his long hair, bushy moustache, squinting eyes and a menacing sneer, he looked more like a highwayman than a farmer. For all Moses knew, Andrew could actually be a bounty hunter. He certainly looked and played the part.

When they reached the Maryland line, Moses changed into a costume of slave rags, a tattered pair of trousers and a torn cotton shirt. "From here on out, we play the game for real," Andrew instructed. He then tightly clamped a pair of handirons around

Moses' wrists. "Now you're my slave," he laughed coldly. Moses was certain he was being double-crossed. Before he could protest, Andrew continued. "If we're stopped, say nothing unless I ask you a question. Remember, I'm a bounty hunter returning you to your master."

After four days in the saddle, they reached the bay. Moses spent the evening gazing across the water. His mind drifted with the ebb tide. He thought about his family on the other side and prayed everything would be as he left it.

Late the next afternoon, a small sailboat ran aground directly in front of camp. "Freedom is in the wind. My sails carry me across the sea of injustice," the sailor declared, jumping from the craft.

"The wind is but the breath of God that sweeps the cause of justice across this land," Andrew replied as his part of the secret code. "Here's your passenger. Remember, I'll wait no more than a day."

"No names are needed," the sailor said to Moses. "Ask anything, but no questions about me or my boat. We'll sail at sunset."

The journey across the bay was calm. The trip reminded Moses of the time he had sailed aboard the Catherine Louise. The sea still had a soothing effect. At last, he was finally going home. While the sailor eyed the wind and the currents, Moses sat back and rehearsed his rescue plan. Down to the smallest detail, he tried to picture the plantation as he last saw it.

Late in the evening, they reached the eastern shore. In the distance, the lights of St. Michael's twinkled brightly. After the boat was dragged onto the beach, Moses received his final instructions.

"We're just northwest of the town, maybe three miles away. From here on out, you're on your own. I'll wait until sunrise. Remember, no more than four passengers."

Moses dashed into the woods. He needed no directions. It seemed like only yesterday, he patrolled this section of the shoreline with his drum at his side, waiting for the British attack.

Two hours later, he was standing behind a tree on the lawn of the manor house. When the last candle was snuffed, he crept to shantytown. Amazingly, everything looked the same; the weathered cabins, the muddy lanes, and the dying campfires. But the darkness was a clever disguise. It was impossible to tell the ill effects of the passing years.

Moses darted in the shadows from cabin to cabin until he reached his home. Crouching low to the ground, he gently pushed open the door without a squeak. In the dancing firelight, he saw the faces of strangers sleeping in beds where his family should have been. He tiptoed to the center of the room and strained his ears for his father's distinctive snore. Nothing sounded the same. My family has been sold down south, he thought.

Reaching down, he cupped the mouth of a slave. "I'm not going to hurt you. I'm looking for Joseph the blacksmith," he whispered.

With a frightened look, the man nervously pointed to a corner of the room where a few fingers of light penetrated the darkness. Moses walked over and gazed down at the wrinkled faced of the grey-haired old man who wheezed with every breath.

"Papa! Papa!" Moses muttered in his father's ear. The old man's eyes slowly opened and then bulged from their sockets as if he had seen a ghost. Before Joseph could utter a word, Moses grabbed him by the arm and led him to the fireplace.

"My Lord!" Joseph gasped. "I'm either dead or dreaming."

"It's me, Moses, in the flesh and blood. I came to take everyone north."

"We got word that you were killed at Fort McHenry, but your mother never believed it. As long as they didn't find your body, she believed you were still alive," said Joseph, caressing his son's face with his bony, shrunken fingers. "I'm afraid I have bad news for you," he said sadly. "Your mother got the fever and died about ten years ago. Your sister was such a good maid, Steele sold her to a plantation in Virginia for a large sum of money. I'm afraid I'm the only one left."

"It can't be. I've come too far to leave empty-handed," Moses barked angrily. "I'm a free man. I have a family and a farm." He pounded his fist into his palm and frowned. This was not how he had planned the rescue. "Then, I'll take you back. At least, you'll have a taste of freedom before you die."

"I'm sorry, son, but I'm too old and sick to be traveling. Things have changed since you left. Everyone, young and old, works the fields. When a slave dies off, they don't buy another. Everyone works harder. Besides, I ain't got much more time here. Any day the Lord will be calling me home. I feel it in my soul. I want to be buried next to your mother, that's where I belong. I'd just be a burden to you . . . "

The conversation was suddenly interrupted by a light in the doorway.

"What's all this noise?" said a haunting voice. "Everyone is supposed to be sleeping."

Moses backed into a corner with his father. A man and a boy entered the cabin and moved toward them. Each carried a musket. The man stopped in front of Moses and held the lantern up to his face.

"Who are you boy?" he demanded. "You're not one of mine. Are you trying to steal one of my slaves?"

"The boy is just looking for his girlfriend, Master Hunt," Joseph interrupted. "He's on his way home. Now go on, I told you there ain't no women here. Now Master Hunt's a fair man, so get out before you get a whipping."

Moses stared in disbelief. He was face to face with a ghost from his past. Yet his father had addressed this demon as Master Hunt. Surely, it was a mistake. When Moses took a step to leave, Hunt slammed him against the wall. Moses threw his hands up in defense. He grabbed Hunt by the throat with both hands and squeezed.

"Don't do it son," Joseph shouted.

Moses relaxed his grip when he felt the cold metal of a musket barrel pressed to his cheek.

"Let him go or I'll shoot," said the boy. Moses dropped his hands and stood motionless. The barrel was now pointed directly under his chin. His dream was turning into a nightmare.

"I don't believe my eyes and ears. Our war hero's come home," Hunted bellowed. "Little Moses, Master's Steele's favorite nigger, is back from the dead. And I suspect he wants back his old job."

"I'm a free man. I don't want any trouble. I want to take my father and leave." Moses said calmly.

"You're still a runaway with a bounty on your head."

"I demand to be taken to Master Steele. He knows business. I'll pay for my father's freedom."

Hunt raised his musket and stepped back. "Things have changed since you left our employment. Old man Steele moved to Baltimore. I'm the master now. I live in the manor house and run the plantation the way I see fit. I'm teaching my son Josh to take over the business."

"Then take me to the town constable for a hearing," Moses yelled in anger. "I demand justice."

Grinding his teeth with a sneer, Hunt leaned close to Moses until their faces touched. "You'll have justice. Tonight, it's just you and me. You forget. We still have a score to settle."

At gun point, Hunt marched Moses and Joseph to the potter's field located in a far corner of the plantation. The mounds of fresh earth bore silent witnesses to Hunt's brutality.

"Get those shovels and start digging," Hunt ordered. We're going to have a family reunion, grandfather, father and son," he howled with a wicked laugh that came from the bowels of hell.

When Joseph picked up the shovel, Moses grabbed him by the arm. "No, Papa," he said. "I'm a free man and I'll die a free man. We won't turn another spade of dirt on this plantation as slaves."

"Have it your way. I'd just as soon leave you to the buzzards," Hunt growled. He raised his rifle to his shoulder and slowly squeezed the trigger. Ka-rack! Sparks flashed as the hammer fell and ignited the powder. As quick as a cat, Joseph jumped in front of Moses. The iron ball pierced his chest and knocked him backwards. Moses caught his father and gently laid him on the ground. Blood spurted from the wound and stained his shirt a dark crimson.

"I hear someone calling me," Joseph said weakly. "I'd best be heading home." His last words trailed off into a faint whisper as his body fell limp.

"One day we'll walk together as free men," cried Moses, kissing his father on the cheek. Jumping to his feet, he yanked the musket from Hunt's hands. He slammed the weapon to the ground and raised his fist behind his ear.

"Shoot him, Josh," screamed Hunt. "Shoot him right now, or

I'll whip you." Joshua sighted the gun on Moses, his hands trembling with fear. Looking into the boy's eyes, Moses slowly lowered his hand and took hold of the musket.

"Hunt, your ways are dying. The boy hasn't learned to hate like you. He sees the evil in all of this madness," said Moses, aiming the gun at Hunt. "Now about that family reunion, Master Hunt. Your slave died a hero and deserves to be buried with honor."

After Hunt carved out a shallow grave, Moses ordered him to remove his clothes and place them on Joseph.

"I think it would be appropriate if we all joined in prayer," announced Moses. "Lord, welcome the soul of Your faithful servant Joseph. His whole life, he dressed in the rags of a slave. Tonight, he comes to You dressed in his finest clothes. Let him walk next to You in the promised land as a free man. Amen."

Moses escorted Hunt and Josh back to the stable where he tied them up. Saddling up a horse, he galloped off into the early morning, hurrying to meet his deadline.

"Just in time," said the sailor. "Sun's getting ready to break the horizon. Anyone else with you?"

"Only me," Moses replied listlessly.

By late morning, the boat beached on the western shore. Andrew was waiting with the horses.

"No chains," said Moses. "I believe the final payment on my freedom has been made." After four days in the saddle, an exhausted Moses arrived home. As he wearily climbed down from his horse, Harriet ran to greet him. She held him to her chest and walked him to the house. From the sadness in his eyes, she knew his dream had not come true.

Chapter Sixteen—

An Honorable Debt

The nightmares ended. Birds flew in the sky. Like Luther, Moses learned to accept the fact that his family was gone. One chapter in his past had been closed. It was time to look to the future. Remembering the teachings of Isaac, Moses turned to his own family. Once again, the Goodwin farm was a place to grow people with tender, loving care.

Days turned to months and months to years all too soon. Over the next decade, the Freeman nest emptied. One by one the girls found husbands and moved away. Only Henry remained on the farm. He was a strapping young man, a spitting image of his father, who loved his work. Locals called him a natural farmer. They said he sprang roots in the soil the day he was born. In 1849, he married a local girl and settled down to work the farm with his father. He loved the land and enjoyed a life filled with hard work and honest labor.

A year later, Henry's first son was born and given the Christian name Moses in honor of his grandfather. From the start, grandfather and grandson were inseparable. Big Moses and Little Moses were their nicknames. The first time Moses held the infant in his arms, the tiny heart vibrated throughout his body. There was a warm, tingling sensation in his fingers when he touched the baby's face. The same feeling he had whenever Isaac had touched him. A strange coincidence or a good omen, Moses debated. He didn't dare mention it to anyone in the family. He was always being chastised for reading too much into everyday occurrences and turning the natural into the supernatural. Big Moses knew a little bit about the supernatural world, or at least, he believed he did. Little

Moses was a special child put on this earth for a special purpose, he reasoned. He could only wonder about the purpose.

At Little Mo's tenth birthday party, Luther cornered Moses and handed him a letter.

"Who's it from?" Moses asked, ripping open the envelope.

"Some old friends," Luther replied haltingly.

Moses unfolded the handwritten letter and began to read:

Dear Mr. Freeman,

I am calling on the foes of slavery to purge this terrible plague from our land. You are welcomed to join me and other men of righteousness. As a man of honor, I offer you the opportunity to repay the favor granted you some years ago. Accept only if you believe in the cause with your body and soul. All around us the armies of good and evil prepare for mortal battle. Together we can end the struggle before vast amounts of blood are spilled in vain.

Your humble servant,

J.B.

"What favor are they talking about?" asked a puzzled Moses, handing the letter to Luther. At first, it sounded like a letter from Reverend Kingston or someone in the church.

"Remember when you tried to rescue your family. I told you someday you might have to repay the favor. I think the time has come.

"And what's this plan to purge the land?"

"I believe the abolitionists want to run a large number of slaves on the underground railroad from plantations in Virginia."

"And who is J.B.?"

"Why I believe that's the captain himself, John Brown."

Moses was stunned. This was the same John Brown who murdered five Kansas slave owners in the name of righteousness. He wondered about the sanity of any man who believed God had appointed him to free the slaves. Moses believed the slavery issue would be peacefully resolved by the end of the decade, but he was in the minority. Race riots around the country boiled the blood of the nation. Moses questioned how much, if any blood, had to be spilled. He firmly believed in the nonviolence philosophy of Isaac.

Slavery was a burning issue, and John Brown was kerosene on the fire.

"I always knew it might come to this someday, but with each passing year the thought became more distant," Moses said solemnly. "I should have known there was no expiration date on this debt."

"What are you going to do?" Luther asked.

"What can I do?" Moses exclaimed in frustration. "I'm just one old man. I can't do anything."

"There's always room for more soldiers in the army of justice. Besides, there's strength in numbers," Luther exhorted. "If the younger ones see two old slaves like us joining the cause, others might follow."

"Two old slaves!" Moses quipped.

"That's right. I said two," Luther shot back. "This time I'm going along. I have to feel I've made my contribution. For years, I've been running slaves through my farm, but the numbers are too small. It's time I repay more of my debt."

Moses nodded his head in agreement. Luther's logic seemed sound. He just hoped he could convince Harriet.

"You want to what?" Harriet screeched. "You and that other old fool are going senile. This battle is for the younger ones to fight."

"You're right," Moses agreed, hoping to win some sympathy. "But I was taught that an honorable man always repays his debts. I cannot refuse to pay mine. There's no need to worry. We're just going to escort some slaves through Maryland."

Harriet saw the troubled look on Moses and knew the answer. "Remember what I told you twenty years ago. It still applies. We've lived full lives. If it is something you truly believe, then you must do it."

"How could I ever forget," Moses whispered. "You and the children are my strength."

The day before he left, Moses walked the barren fields. The October morning was cold and cloudy. A ghostly silence filled the air. The sky was empty. Strangely enough, he had not seen a bird for days. It reminded him of the time he attempted to rescue his family. Only this time, there were no good omens to be found.

Later, he spent an hour talking with Henry about the farm. It proved meaningless. No one knew the farm better than Henry. Everything was in good hands until he returned.

Despite the reassurances from Luther and Harriet, Moses had a feeling of gloom and doom. If he didn't make it back, he worried about the legacy that would be passed down to future generations of Freemans. There was the farm, but it carried no significance with the history of his family. Likewise, there were no family heirlooms which had special meaning. Everything was from the Goodwins. What do I have that could be the symbol of the Freeman family, he fretted. He thought long and hard as he tapped his fingers on the table. Unconsciously, he drummed the military commands from decades ago. "Why, of course. The answer was there all the time. Only a drumbeat away," he said with a sense of satisfaction.

In the afternoon, Moses climbed to the attic. Carrying a small pouch of woodworking tools, he rummaged through the piles of household junk. Years ago, Harriet told him she found the drum, but Moses just shrugged it off. At least the drum wasn't kindling, he thought at the time.

In a far corner behind a curtain of cobwebs, Moses located Lillian's steamer trunk. He gently removed the drum and cradled it in his hands. Like its owner, the drum was showing its age. Time had darkened the shell, covering it with a layer of dirt and dust.

"If only you could talk," he said. "Oh, the stories you could tell." Using his shirt sleeve, he dusted off the black eagle. "I'm sorry I have neglected you, my friend, but I still believe in your power. Now you can be my messenger."

He placed the drum between his legs, removed the heads and began carving. An hour or so later, the job was finished. The drum was returned to its resting place. The final task had been completed. Moses was ready to meet his fate.

The next morning Moses and Luther headed south for Chambersburg, Pennsylvania. Two days later, they arrived at an abandoned quarry on the edge of town. Their contact was waiting.

"Gentlemen, I'm the captain's shipping agent," greeted the

man. "Tomorrow we ride for Harper's Ferry. That's all I can tell you. You'll get more details there."

On the evening of October 16th, the men arrived at a small farmhouse, five miles west of Harper's Ferry on the Maryland side of the Potomac River. Moses glanced over his shoulder with every move. He was extremely conscious of the fact that he was no longer in Pennsylvania. Maryland was in the Union but probably held more Confederates than Yankees. Technically, he and Luther were slaves once again. They couldn't be overly cautious. As they waited in the orchard behind the house, a lone figure approached.

Gentlemen, my name is John Brown," the stranger said, extending a long, thin hand. "It is an honor to have you join us."

"No, Mr. Brown. The honor is ours," replied Luther excitedly, obviously flattered to meet the man he thought would end slavery. Moses was merely polite, impressed but not infatuated. Without taking his eyes off Brown's face, he shook hands. The famous abolitionist stood tall and lean like an old pine tree. With a full head of hair and a white beard, he looked more like a prophet than a madman. His steely gray eyes were bright and strong, but deadly cold.

"You're just in time. Tonight, we move," Brown added. "I plan to seize the arsenal at Harper's Ferry and then liberate the nearby plantations. We will form a slave army and begin the great revolution. You will stay at the farm and organize the slaves as they are freed."

"But what can two old men do?" Moses asked, shocked at the boldness of the plan. "We'd be more of a hindrance than a help?"

"Mr. Freeman, the soul of this nation is in the hands of all of its citizens," Brown implored in a deep, resonant voice. It matters not if you're young or old, man or woman. This army has a place for every recruit. The will of the people shall overcome."

As Brown headed back, Moses turned to Luther. "Did you hear what he said?" Moses asked nervously. "He's going to attack the United States arsenal. We'll be hung for treason. What ever happened to running freight on the underground railroad? He thinks thousands of slaves are going to follow him. You know those slaves are going to be afraid to take one step off the plantation. Freedom is not a word in their vocabulary."

Moses remembered the slave uprisings from the newspapers. They were as short-lived as their leaders. The names of Gabriel Prosser in Virginia in 1800, Charles Deslondes in Louisiana in 1811, Denmark Vesey in South Carolina in 1822, and, the most recent, Nat Turner in Virginia in 1831 came to mind. All shot or hung. He feared the names of Moses Freeman and Luther Walker in Maryland would be the headline in 1859.

"Maybe, that's the point," Luther insisted. "The captain wants us to help the slaves. What better teachers than us. We wear the clothes of experience. There's not a soldier here with a better uniform. Look, we've come this far. Let's see what happens."

As they walked toward the farmhouse, Luther added one last thought. "You know I can remember a time when you didn't know the meaning of freedom. It seems like you needed a teacher if my memory is correct. Maybe, you need to go back to school."

Moses smiled weakly and hung his head in shame. He had no right to chastise Luther. Generations of his people had been waiting for this day. Of course, he would be willing to sacrifice his freedom, even his life, if necessary.

At around 8 P.M., Brown and eighteen of his men marched from the Kennedy farm to Harper's Ferry. Moses and Luther walked a few steps behind the group. Although, they weren't included in the strike force, Brown allowed them to join the march. He was more than glad to muster all the men he could. Moses' interest in the march was strictly self-serving. He desperately needed to see how this "Provisional Army of the United States" operated. He had given his word he would help, so there was no turning back. But if John Brown was hell-bent on a suicide mission, he wanted to be prepared.

The captain, wore his "Kansas cap," a peaked cap with hanging earflaps, given to him by an Ottawa Indian chief. He drove the wagon loaded with pikes, a crowbar, a sledgehammer, and kindling material for igniting fires. The troops wore long shawls to ward off the chilly evening and conceal their Sharps carbines. When they reached the covered railroad bridge across the Potomac River, Moses and Luther were dismissed. As they retraced their steps, they heard the heavy boots pound a slow, but steady cadence against the thick timbers on the bridge. The great revolution was about to begin.

Back at the cabin, Moses and Luther rejoined the four men who comprised the rear guard. Their mission was to await orders to transport weapons or arm the slaves. Unable to sleep, Moses talked late into the night with Owen Brown, the son who was left behind because of his withered arm. It was a revealing conversation. John Brown was a fanatic but no fool. From his soapbox, he preached an end to slavery and practiced what he preached. For years, he had prepared for the armed conflict between slaves and slave owners. The town of Harper's Ferry had been carefully selected. Despite the fervor of Owen and his father, Moses wasn't convinced they were doing the right thing. He believed in the message but not in messenger. Certainly, the method of delivery was suspect.

At daybreak, the men were up and about, nervously pacing about the small rooms. The night had been filled with fitful sleep. They anxiously waited for word from Harper's Ferry. A report was overdue. Late in the morning, the wagon rumbled down the lane. Three young Negroes who had been liberated during the night were sitting behind the driver. The men dashed from the cabin for the latest news.

"We have seized the arsenal and have begun freeing slaves. The captain will signal when he is ready for the rear guard to advance," said the driver. "We need to start moving supplies to the schoolhouse."

"Tell my father, there is no rear guard. No slaves found their way to the farm during the night," Owen pleaded.

"The slaves will be coming. That's why we need to move the weapons to a convenient supply point. It's only a mile from town. We'll be able to arm everyone much quicker."

The wagon was loaded with more weapons. When it disappeared down the road, Moses and Luther looked at each other with a pained expression. Everything was going as planned, but disaster was lurking around the corner. Moses and Luther saw it coming. No slaves meant no army. No army meant no revolution. No revolution meant no end to slavery.

Hours later, the wagon returned for another load. This time

Luther volunteered to ride along and help unload. The revolution was in the hands of the people, and Luther was sitting on his. He was willing to aid the cause in any way he could. Secretly, he hoped the Captain would ask him to join the raid.

The remaining men returned to the cabin and waited. For hours, Moses sat by the window and watched the rain. The dreary day reflected the mood of the rear echelon. The weather forecast offered no relief. Moses didn't foresee a bright outlook for either the weather or the raid on Harper's Ferry.

Late in the afternoon, a lone horseman approached. Moses saw the black man and was encouraged. He assumed that legions of slaves would be arriving shortly. Brandishing a fancy shotgun under his arm, the rider sounded the alarm.

"Our men are trapped in the engine house. At daybreak, the militia will storm the building. We must join the fight at once if we are to save them," warned the rider.

"Who are you?" Owen asked. "You are not one of my father's men."

"I was freed this morning."

"And how many men are with my father."

"Ten, maybe twenty." Owen shook his head in disgust. The numbers were too small. Failure to recruit a slave army had doomed his father. He had to rescue him. His only chance was to attack that night. His only hope was that more slaves were being armed at the schoolhouse.

Owen gave the order to abandon the cabin. Maps and papers were thrown into the fire. Men scrambled about the house collecting as many weapons as they could carry. Outside in the driving rain, they formed a single column and marched. At dusk, they reached the one-room schoolhouse.

"Your father and his men are still trapped in the engine house. Your brothers have been mortally wounded. A few men have been captured," the guard solemnly informed Owen. "All we can do now is escape."

"How can this be?" Owen asked, his face turning ashen. "I still hear gunshots coming from the town."

"Just the local boys celebrating. I suppose the shooting will go on all night long."

Owen decided to wait another hour. As minutes ticked away, he hastily sketched a battle plan on the back of an envelope. He was certain that thousands of liberated slaves were marching to the schoolhouse. When the hour passed, he reluctantly gave the order.

"Victory has been denied us today. God has another plan to cleanse the plague from our land. Rest assured, what we have accomplished will be recognized by the world. One day, we will fight again. We start immediately for Chambersburg. Take nothing for granted. We are fugitives from the law."

As the men prepared to set out, Moses approached Owen. "I must go back for my friend. We've traveled the same road for many years. The journey cannot end like this. I must find him, even if it means risking my life."

"I understand," Owen replied with a look of despair. "In my heart, I feel I should go back for my father, but I must save the rest of the men. Do what your heart tells you. May our paths cross again someday."

Moses crept along the riverbank until he sighted the railroad bridge. From a safe distance, he surveyed his situation. At best, it was bleak. To prevent sabotage, armed guards had been posted along the structure. Four armed guards huddled near the entrance on the Maryland side. Surely, there was at least the same number on the other side.

Moses was frustrated. What could one old man do against an army. Climbing the bridge was too risky. Overpowering the guards required more men. Swimming across the rising river was simply suicide. The town was only a couple hundred yards away, but it might as well had been a thousand. Moses quickly concluded it was time for a new plan. But there was a silver lining in this dark cloud. Owen was lucky he didn't get the chance to test his military tactics. He and his men would have been slaughtered.

Moses retreated upriver. He searched unsuccessfully for a shallow gap where he could ford the river. Every place he checked, the river was too wide and too deep. About a mile from the bridge, he stumbled across a small rowboat which had been hidden in the weeds. Too dark to see, he ran his hands along the sides and bottom. No holes or missing planks. The boat seemed seaworthy. There were even two oars stowed inside. Certainly, an odd place to find a boat, but, nevertheless, an answer to his prayers.

Even with a boat, the crossing would be difficult. Heavy rains swelled the river to a flood level. The rising water hid the massive boulders which could splinter the boat in seconds. But there was no time for second guessing. Moses knew this was his only chance. He quietly slid the boat into the river. Something rustled in the weeds. Moses froze. Nothing but the wind or the rain, he thought. He lifted his leg to climb aboard.

"Psst! Psst! Mr. Moses. It's me, Jesse." A shadowy figure emerged from the tall grass. Moses was shocked to see the young black man who had appeared at the farm. The menacing sneer was a toothy smile, but the shotgun was still cradled in his arms.

"I thought you went with the others," Moses said. "Why the change of heart?"

"Mr. Moses, I've only been a free man for a day, and I can tell you it's a good feeling. But if I can't free the others, then my freedom means nothing. Now don't get me wrong, I like being free, but you know how. . ."

"Say no more. I know how it is. And the boat?"

"One of Mr. Brown's men hid it here this afternoon."

"And my friend Luther. Did you see him?"

"I saw him this afternoon walking near the bridge."

"Then he could still be alive," Moses said hopefully. "Climb aboard. I need all the help I can get."

The crossing was extremely dangerous. Even with two men rowing, the current carried the boat downriver. Luckily, the river beached them at a spot just north of the town. They pulled the boat ashore and waited to see if they had been spotted. When the coast was clear, they crawled on their hands and knees until they reached the edge of town. From there, they stalked the alleys, hoping to find a clue about the prisoners. When they reached the main thoroughfare, they crouched in a doorway and listened. Bang! Bang-bang! Shots rang out as drunken soldiers spilled from the taverns and staggered in the streets.

"They held Mr. Thompson in the hotel before they shot him," Jesse said, pointing to a tall building across the street.

"It's a good place to start looking," Moses replied.

The two men dashed across the street and ran into the alley behind the hotel. As they hid behind some barrels, two soldiers exited the roadhouse and milled around the back door. They passed a jug and talked loudly.

"I've got to guard the prisoner," said one of the soldiers in a slurred voice. "They ought to just shoot the poor Negro tonight so everyone can celebrate. It doesn't make much sense to keep him alive. We'll just take him out tomorrow and shoot him. Maybe, I'll shoot him tonight and get myself a medal."

"That could be your friend they're talking about," Jesse whispered.

"Or it could be one of Brown's men," Moses offered. "But it's worth the gamble to find out."

When the jug emptied, the men departed. One soldier walked down the alley while the other entered the hotel and walked upstairs. Sliding their backs against the wall, Moses and Jesse inched their way to the door. Once inside, they found themselves in a hallway next to the hotel's tavern. Only a few feet away on the other side of the wall, soldiers were celebrating their victory with song and drink.

"Where do we go from here?" asked Jesse.

"Follow me." Moses directed as he motioned with his finger. "I have a plan that just might work." Grabbing a uniform hat and jacket from a coat rack, Moses tiptoed his way up the stairs. Jesse followed hard on his heels. Peering around the corner on the second floor, Moses spotted the soldier. He was slumped in a chair with his rifle between his legs and his cap pulled down over his eyes.

"I think he's sleeping. Let's rush him," said Jesse.

"Too dangerous," Moses cautioned. "If we startle him, he might start shooting. The army would be here in seconds." Moses pulled the cap over his eyebrows and flung the jacket across his shoulders. "Give me your gun and start walking slowly down the hall." Moses placed the gun at Jesse's back and began barking orders. "Get up them steps, boy, or I'll fill you with buckshot." Moses stooped behind Jesse so that only the top of his cap was visible. The loud voice startled the guard who clumsily jumped to his feet. Before he could challenge the two strangers, Moses spoke.

"The sergeant ordered me to deliver this prisoner. Caught him near the bridge. Take good care of him. He's a runaway who might be worth some money."

Moses and Jesse moved closer. When the guard finally realized the escort was another Negro, it was too late. In a split second, Moses pushed Jesse aside and lunged forward. The guard opened his mouth to scream, but stopped abruptly. He relaxed his jaw and bit his lower lip as the barrel of the shotgun settled underneath his chin.

"Not a whisper, or I'll blow your head clean off," Moses sneered. "Now let's go inside."

The guard nodded and opened the door. In the center of the room, Luther sat bound and gagged. After being untied, he updated the day's events. "The captain and seven of his men are barricaded in the engine house. Both of his boys have been shot. Federal troops are arriving tonight from Washington. At daybreak, they'll storm the building."

"It's too late for them but not for us. We've got to hurry," Moses warned. "Follow us. We have a boat at the edge of town."

They lashed the guard to the chair and raced down the stairs. Bursting through the back door, they sprinted down the alley. There was no time to be cautious. At least for a few seconds, the element of surprise was on their side. Moses still had the shotgun. Anybody who got in their way was a dead man. He hoped none of these part-time soldiers was willing to take the chance. They were a block away from the hotel when they heard the uproar.

"The prisoner has escaped. All men to your posts," came the cry.

Footsteps hammered the cobblestone as soldiers fanned out across the town.

"There they are," came a shout followed by a rifle shot.

Jesse surged ahead of the old men as they raced to the river. Breathing heavily and gasping for air, Moses and Luther slowed to a trot. Their age had caught up with them before the soldiers.

"We're almost there," cheered Jesse. "You can't stop now. They'll shoot you dead whether you're running or standing."

Moses and Luther picked up the pace but were losing the race. The footsteps behind them grew louder. They reached the river just seconds ahead of the soldiers. Plung! Pling! Plung! Shots peppered the water as the three men dove into the boat. Leaning over the sides, Moses and Jesse grabbed the oars and paddled furiously. When the boat floundered, bullets rained like hailstones.

"Give me those damn oars, or you'll get us all killed," Luther shouted as he moved to the center seat. He grabbed the oars and with a few mighty strokes moved the boat forward. "If I can row across the Chesapeake in a squall, I can row through any storm." The boat plowed ahead into the darkness. A few more strokes and they would be safe. Water splashed wildly. Luther grunted and groaned with each mighty stroke. Suddenly, he dropped the oars and slumped forward. "I've been hit," he cried out painfully.

Moses grabbed Luther by the arm and pulled him to the bottom of the boat. "Just a flesh wound. You'll be standing behind the plow in a week or two," he said calmly. He gawked at the blood gushing from Luther's chest. He knew the wound was fatal.

"Looks like I crossed the river once too often. Next river I'll be crossing is the Jordan," Luther groaned with a forced smile. He squeezed Moses by the hand. "Promise me you'll take me home to be buried. I want to die a free man."

"I promise, dear friend. You're going home where you'll be a free man forever."

Instead of carrying the boat downriver, the currents pushed it back to shore. The soldiers again took aim. Bullets splintered the gunwales. Wooden planks disintegrated from the relentless barrage. Moses and Jesse huddled on the bottom, hoping the boat would catch the current again before it sank.

"Mr. Moses. If I'm going to die, I'm also going to die a free man. It's my turn to save us," Jesse shouted frantically. Without another word, he made his move and reached for the oars. Thwump! A bullet ripped through his stomach. He fell to his knees and rocked back and forth in a futile attempt to grab one of the oars.

"God Almighty, help us now," Moses implored when he saw Jesse slump over the side. Things were getting worse by the second. He had to take a chance and save the boat. He jumped up and shielded Jesse from the gunfire. Grabbing hold of the swing-ing oars, he rowed madly. The boat scooted across the river. A few more strokes and it would catch the current.

Pa-ting! Moses dropped the oars and clutched his thigh. When he looked at his hand, it was covered with blood. The wound felt like a bee sting, but he was too scared to feel any real pain. If he didn't act quickly, there would be more than one hole in his body.

"Our only chance is in the water," he shouted.

"I don't know how to swim," Jesse moaned.

"Standing or swimming, it doesn't matter. They'll kill us ei-ther way."

Moses tackled Jesse at the chest, knocking both men into the river. Plung! Plung-Plung-Plung! Bullets churned the surface where they splashed. Seconds later, scarlet stains boiled to the surface. The rowboat spun wildly out of control and smashed against the rocks. The body of Luther spilled into the river and washed ashore.

Moses sank to the bottom of the swirling river like a rock. He opened his eyes and saw nothing. The water was as black and cold as the night. Strangely, he didn't panic. Something rather remarkable was happening. He closed his eyes as a wave of tran-quility caressed his body. His life flashed before him in a series of photographs. At one point, he saw himself as a young boy being tossed from a rocky ledge into a deep pool of water.

That image sparked his soul. The rage which burned deep inside had been stoked. No amount of water, not even a river, could extinguish the inferno. All the hate he had seen in his life-time exploded. He refused to die a slave. "I survived the water once. I can survive it again," he told himself. With his last ounce of strength, he kicked his legs and flapped his arms. When his head broke the surface, he gulped for air and frantically waved his arms.

"My drum. Where is the drum?" he cried out in despair before being pulled under by the current.

The soldiers on the riverbank dropped their rifles and laughed. They savored every moment of this cruel spectacle. A well-placed bullet would end their folly too soon.

"Look at that old drunken fool," one soldier cackled. "Call-ing for his rum while drowning in the middle of the river."

At daybreak, a company of U.S. Marines under the command of Lieutenant Robert E. Lee stormed the engine house and captured John Brown. The local militia spent the day searching the river for bodies. Three days later, a telegraph message reached Hope Springs. Reverend Kingston carried the message to Harriet and Mildred.

Location: Baltimore and Ohio Railroad Office, Harper's Ferry Depot, October 18, 1859
Subject: River Accident at Harper's Ferry.

Amid the chaos of John Brown's attack on the federal armory at Harper's Ferry, a tragic accident occurred on the Potomac River last night. Three Negro men drowned when their fishing boat was crushed against the rocks in a flood surge. One victim was identified by personal papers as Luther Walker, a free black from Hope Springs, Pennsylvania. His body is being transported home. The bodies of the others have not been recovered. The undertaker reported that drowning victims often remain submerged for months due to river currents. Efforts to recover the bodies will continue when the weather improves.

Reverend Kingston conducted the memorial service for Luther and Moses. Though hobbled by age and failing health, he still preached the word of the Lord with fire and brimstone. During the eulogy, he praised the two former slaves who knew the true meaning of freedom.

"Lord, what a fine morning to be in your kingdom," he said in a booming voice which reached to the heavens. "No doubt your pastures are greener with the help of Luther and Moses. No longer do they toil on this earthly plain as slaves. For today, they work your fields as free men. They traveled the long, hard road to freedom. It was a righteous path which led to your door. You were their eternal hope; now their eternal salvation. You freed their bodies and then their souls. We thank you and pray you will do the same for us one day. Lord, it's a fine day to be free. Today, Luther and Moses are free. Free at last. Free forever."

Luther was buried beneath a tall, oak tree on his farm. At the request of Harriet, no marker was erected for Moses.

"As long as there's no tomb, there will be no tombstone," she declared defiantly. "If he washed downriver, then I'm sure the Almighty God carried his body across the ocean to the shores of his native land where he will rest in peace forever," she professed adamantly.

Family members honored her wish. They were never sure if she truly believed Moses was still alive. They merely accepted it as her way of dealing with the death of a loved one.

Chapter Seventeen–

Thunder at Gettysburg

The spring of 1863 marked a season of promise for Henry and the Freeman family. After three disastrous crops, he believed this would be the year of a plentiful harvest. The farm had survived without Moses but not without good weather. It may have been superstition, coincidence or natural phenomenon, but since Moses had been gone, the weather refused to cooperate. Summers were too short and hot for a good growing season; winters too long and too cold for an early planting. A prolonged drought made water scarce. Ponds and streams dried up into puddles.

The only things Henry could pour into the fields were his sweat and the bank's money. It was going to be a close race to see which ran out first. Every year he was forced to borrow from the bank to make up for the losses. He was running out of seasons. Most likely, this would be his last. Already, the bank was suggesting an auction to cover the loans. The last thing in the world Henry wanted to lose was the farm. The land was the only family heirloom.

Henry was not alone in his predicament. Every other farmer in the region was on the brink of financial ruin, but didn't seem to care. The weather was rarely mentioned. The great Civil War was on everyone's lips. One of these days it's going to rain, people surmised, but they weren't so sure when the Union Army would win a major battle. General Robert E. Lee and his Confederate Army continually rallied the South with a string of impressive victories. On the other side, Union generals displayed a knack of turning victory into stalemate and stalemate into defeat. Lee was even willing to take the fight north into Maryland. Every Pennsylvanian feared their state was next. Any day, they expected a knock on the door from a Confederate raiding party.

In the colored community, all of the talk was about the Fifty-Fourth Massachusetts Regiment, the first recognized black unit in the Union. President Lincoln's Emancipation Proclamation on January 1, 1863 not only freed the slaves but opened up the ranks of the military to Negroes. Most colored folks expected a massive Negro army to simply overrun the Confederates. They bet the war would end within the year. Needless to say, they were completely out of touch with reality. They talked possibilities not politics. Black units were a novelty, a public relations campaign for the war effort. They were lucky if they had uniforms.

Henry was not so confident. While he occasionally fantasized about joining a colored regiment, he knew his place was on the farm. He was more interested in dirt than death. Being head of the family was more than a title. It was a duty he took seriously. Besides, if he did fight, he wasn't so sure about the outcome. While he despised the South, he distrusted the motives of the North. If the Union Army was so confident of victory why did they need black soldiers to fight the war. From reading the newspapers, it appeared as if President Lincoln was running out of white men to slaughter.

Talk about the war always had Henry thinking about John Brown's raid. Prophet or madman, it made no difference. John Brown had predicted the orgy of bloodshed before he walked to the gallows. Forget Fort Sumter, Harper's Ferry was the first battle of the war. Henry found it quite remarkable, if not unbelievable, that his father had played a part in this monumental event. From the beginning, he doubted the story about the fishing accident. When the local undertaker found a bullet hole in Luther's chest, he knew it was a lie.

Henry did a little detective work of his own. Although the survivors were reluctant to talk, he pieced together a rather accurate account of that night. One day the truth would prevail. His father and Luther would be rightfully acclaimed as freedom fighters. But until that time, everyone in the Freeman family spoke in hushed tones about the incident. While the name of John Brown was taboo in the family household, the war was debated with fervor. The Fifty-Fourth Massachusetts Regiment was always a headline topic.

"Mother, I need to talk to you. It's very important," Henry said with a tone of urgency.

"Now I've told you time and time again. The crops will be better this year. You need a little more faith in prayer than the plow," Harriet kidded good-naturedly.

"It's not the farm. It's Little Moses. He has this foolish idea about joining the army. All he talks about is that black regiment up north. I keep telling him he's too young, but he says he can sign up as a drummer boy."

Harriet closed her eyes and rocked in her chair. "Your father was a drummer when he was a young man," she said wistfully. "He never told me much about it because I disliked his African ways. Looking back, perhaps, it wasn't a good idea. Every man needs to know his past." She suddenly stopped rocking, leaned forward and grabbed Henry's hand. "Of all the books your father read, I never let him read his own history. I never let him pass down his family heritage. You inherited your father's love for the land, but how much do you know about his past."

"Very little," Henry replied. "But how does all of this affect Little Moses?"

"Your son is thirteen years old now and a fine young man. He works with you in the fields, but I can see his heart is not in the farm. He's afraid to say anything to you because he loves you too much to hurt your feelings. There comes a time when every bird leaves the nest. If you don't give him your blessing, you might regret it for the rest of your life.

"Maybe you're right. Maybe, it's time for him to write his own history," Henry said, trying to convince himself that letting Little Mo join the army was the right thing. "He's as stubborn as a mule. He'd probably run away and join anyhow."

"Every man is a book of wisdom. Experience is the ink which fills those blank pages. I'm sure he'll do fine, if that's what he wants," Harriet reassured him.

That evening Henry sat down with his son and explained the harsh conditions for a Negro soldier. Low pay, meager rations, filthy quarters, secondhand uniforms, broken equipment, and the scorn of many white soldiers were guaranteed. And God forbid what would happened, if he was ever captured by the Confederates. Little Moses was undaunted. His dream of being a drummer boy burned brighter than ever. The fire in his soul would not be extinguished.

The next week Henry signed the enlistment papers. He was relieved to learn that Moses would be assigned to a black unit in Washington. After training, he would be permanently detailed to guard duty in the city. Not a bad situation, Henry decided. Little Moses would be close to home and far from the enemy.

For the farewell dinner, Harriet prepared a feast which rivaled Christmas. While everyone finished dessert, she pulled Little Moses aside.

"Follow me," she said leading the way to the attic. She went straight to Lillian's trunk, pulled out the burlap bag, and handed it to Little Moses. "Take this as a gift on your enlistment. I believe your grandfather wanted you to have this someday. It was his heritage. For too many years, it stayed hidden. Now is the time to share the secret of our history."

As the 77th New York Infantry trampled across the field below Cemetery Ridge, the order was given to bivouac for the night. The weary members of Company A dropped to their knees, opened their knapsacks, and devoured the remaining salt pork and hardtack from their three-day ration. While soldiers removed their wool jackets and boots, band members stowed away their instruments and set out to fetch wood and water. The regiment had been on the march for two days. They were the last reinforcements to reach the town of Gettysburg, Pennsylvania. If lucky, they would be the last ones called to the front line. The initial reports were not promising. The battle had been raging a day and a half with unbelievable casualties.

Moses and Billy, the youngest drummer boys in the band, were quick to recover from the physical ordeal. Their feet weren't tired and sore. It was their fingers and wrists that needed rest. For nearly two straight days, they paced the endless march with their drumming.

"At the rate we're marching through Pennsylvania, I'll be home by the end of the week," Moses said, pulling paper and pencil from his knapsack. It had been over four months since he enlisted. Unfortunately, his family was unable to visit. It was simply too dangerous to travel south under any conditions. Instead, he wrote home, at least once a month.

"If you hurry up and finish that letter, we can walk to the top of the ridge and maybe see your home," Billy replied impatiently.

"I've got to write my folks and tell them I'm in a new unit. They think I'm back in Washington."

"Don't worry. We'll be back in a few days. Just as soon as we scare the Rebs away."

The boys raced up the sloping hill. At the top of the ridge, they stood in silent awe at the spectacle before them. The entire Civil War unfolded before their eyes. Thousands of infantrymen lined the ridge as far as the eye could see. Gun crews manned hundreds of artillery pieces. Across the valley, just about a mile away, their Confederate counterparts stood ready. Everyone waited for the order to start the battle.

The afternoon heat muffled the cannon fire coming from the south. Clouds of black and white smoke hung in the distance like a fog. Shouts echoed along the valley from the left flank about a mile and a half away. There the gallant men of the 20th Maine were engaged in fierce hand to hand combat with Confederates who were attempting to take the high ground at Little Roundtop. Down in the valley, charges and countercharges left The Peach Orchard and The Wheatfield strewn with the bodies of more than 4,000 dead and wounded. Meanwhile, a force of 1,600 Rebels, rushing to fill a gap on the Union line, were turned back with a bayonet charge from the 1st Minnesota, a group of 262 men. A half a mile away on the right flank, Union forces dug in at Culp's Hill and fought off Confederate charges which would last into the night. All around the valley, a maelstrom of blood soaked the ground. Like the eye of a hurricane, the center of the ridge was calm.

"Come on Billy. Let's get back," Moses implored. Although Moses was nervous about leaving camp, he knew nothing would be said as long as he was with Billy Young, the unit mascot. Corporal William Young at age fourteen was a grizzled war veteran. His reputation rivaled that of Johnny Clem, the famous "drummer boy of Shiloh," who reportedly shot a Confederate colonel out of the saddle. In September 1862, at the Battle of Antietam, the bloodiest day of the war, William was dubbed "Billy Yank" for his heroism. He single-handedly captured a Confederate scout and saved his unit from being overrun.

The men of the 77th would rather go into battle without their rifles than their good luck charm. Good ole' "Billy Yank" was one of the toughest drummers in the Union army. He drank coffee, smoked a pipe, spit tobacco juice and swore with the best. There wasn't a better drummer in the army. For that matter, there wasn't a better friend either.

Although Moses was a new man in the unit, Billy took him under his wing and taught him about the army. He spent hours teaching him the drum cadences for "forming the ranks" and "skirmishers on line."

If Moses wanted to be a drummer, then, by God, Billy would teach him to be the second best drummer in the army. Moses was a "good guy" who deserved a chance to make it, reckoned Billy. And besides, it was nice to have somebody his own age for a pal.

Billy made Moses follow him like a shadow. More important than any drum lesson, he showed Moses how to survive in the white man's army. Learning who to see, where to go and what to do were essential skills, just as important as firing a rifle. The way Billy figured it, Moses had to learn how to fight his own army before he fought the Rebs. The strategy worked extremely well.

Moses realized he was finally accepted because of Billy, but he never took advantage of the friendship. Whenever the regiment marched, he took pride when someone from the ranks called out for "Salt and Pepper" to sound the drums. It was a good nickname for two good friends.

Back at camp, soldiers meticulously cleaned their weapons and rested. After dinner, they gossiped around the campfire. They responded with dark humor to the latest battlefield reports. Their turn to dance with the devil was only hours away.

"Hot! Too damn hot to fight a war," said one of the soldiers.

"Doesn't make much sense with us sitting around a fire in wool uniforms. Only makes things hotter," came the quick response.

"It's so hot. It's like hell's coming up to meet us," the first soldier lamented.

"At least we're in the right spot," the second commented. "Won't have far to go for anything. The cemetery's right up the road and hell is right underfoot. Only thing I'm going to hate is those long lines. The devil's going to be real busy with all of them Johnny Rebs waiting to see him. Might even give me a chance to sneak out and head in the other direction."

Following a chorus of laughter, the voices fell silent. All of the men wondered if that would be their fate. No doubt, the Rebs were thinking the same thing just across the valley.

In the shadows of the fire, Moses and Billy stretched out in the soft grass and did their own talking.

"You're awfully quiet tonight, Billy Yank," Moses prodded.

"I'm just thinking," Billy replied whimsically. "I've got this funny feeling about tomorrow. I don't think Johnny Reb is going to run from this battle. He's going to run right up our gut."

"We'll find out tomorrow when we get our orders."

"That's why I'm worried. I don't want to go to the hospital. I'd rather be on the line fighting the living than picking up the dead. Did I ever tell you about Antietam?"

"Well, not exactly," Moses stammered with surprise. Now he definitely knew something was wrong. Billy never told war stories, especially stories about himself.

"I worked burial detail outside the surgeon's tent. Picked up arms and legs by the bucket full. It ain't going to happen again. What I do best is drum. I can whip any drummer in both armies. Tomorrow, I'm drumming on the ridge or leaving."

"You, the orphan drummer who calls the army home, are deserting," replied a startled Moses.

"Not deserting, just quitting. There's a difference. And one more thing," Billy continued. "Promise me you'll take care of my drum. It's all I have in the world. If anything happens to me, I want you to have it. Consider it a gift from your friend Billy Yank."

"I always wanted a new drum, but I don't think I want it that way," Moses said with a chuckle, trying to ease Billy's fear. "I'd rather win it in a card game. At least, you'll be able to see it. Might even let you play it."

"Private Freeman," the sergeant called out. "The captain wants to see you in his tent right away." Moses jumped to his feet, straightened his uniform and ran down the hill. He was sure the captain would reprimand him for being on the ridge without permission.

Captain Reed Brookes, the well-mannered and soft-spoken college professor, seemed like the ideal officer to Moses. Although only in his mid-twenties, he had the wisdom of a well-seasoned veteran. While he distanced himself from the other soldiers, he took a special liking to the drum corps, especially his two young drummers. His fatherly approach always made allowances for their youthful enthusiasm and indiscretions. It was the perfect mix for Moses and Billy.

"Private Freeman reporting as ordered, sir."

"Come in and have a seat, private. I'll be with you in a minute." Moses stood at ease while the captain huddled over some papers at his field desk. After a heavy sigh, Brookes dropped his pen, removed his glasses, and looked up.

"Tomorrow we expect an attack on the center of the ridge. I'm sorry to say that I cannot guarantee your safety on the battlefield. You could be shot on sight by a sharpshooter, or sold as a slave if captured. As the only Negro soldier in the company, you have gained the respect of every officer and enlisted man. After weighing all the factors, I have decided to assign you to the field hospital. You will report tomorrow after breakfast."

Moses was shocked by the captain's order. Grisly images of arms and legs piling up to the sky flooded his mind. Billy's prediction was coming true.

"Please captain," Moses pleaded. "I would prefer to stay on the ridge. I've proven myself on the parade field, now I have to prove myself on the battlefield."

Brookes leaned back and reconsidered. Throughout his career, he witnessed the hardships endured by the black regiments. He admired their tenacity. If ever he had the chance, he vowed to give them their day in battle. No one deserved the opportunity more than Moses, even if he was only thirteen years old. Boys his age and younger picked cotton from sunrise to sunset.

"Very well, private. I can't argue with your logic. You have earned the right to decide your fate. If that's what you want, so be it. Remember, you can change your mind at anytime."

After Moses left, Brookes finished his letter to his father.

Gettysburg, July 3, 1863

Dear Father,

It's been very difficult to write as the regiment has been on the move. We've been tracking General Lee north through Maryland and rather unfortunately, have met him at a little town in southern Pennsylvania called Gettysburg. The fighting began two days ago. Casualties have been extremely high.

The weather has remained hot throughout the campaign. No breeze blows across the fields to clear the stench of the dead. No rain cleanses the blood from the soil. Perhaps, tomorrow's sacrifice will appease the gods of war and offer some relief.

To a more interesting matter, I would like to address the conduct of one of my soldiers. Moses Freeman is a drummer in the band. Not so unusual, except for the fact that he is one of the few Negroes at Gettysburg. The boy endures barbaric torments for being of his race. Yet somehow he rises above the injustice and proves himself the better man. He plays a battered drum that looks like a relic from the Revolution and speaks in reverent tones about his grandfather who fought against the British. Quite possibly, just a tall tale from the imagination of a child. But there is something about his sincerity that tells me differently.

When I gather more information, perhaps, you can do some research. I'm sure a stuffy, old history professor like yourself would welcome the opportunity. Hopefully, the Almighty will allow me to write next week.

In two days, the nation will celebrate its independence. I pray to God the fireworks at Gettysburg will be silenced by then.

Your loving son,
Reed

Moses hurried back to tell Billy the good news, but found him sound asleep next to his drum. Moses picked up the heirloom and examined every detail as he had done a hundred times before. Billy's parade drum was the finest instrument in the land. The maple shell measured fourteen inches in diameter and sixteen inches in depth. Inside the drum, the maker's label read: *Union Manufacturing Company, 184 West Baltimore Street, Baltimore, Mary-*

land. On the front was a bald eagle with a white crown, perched underneath an arching cloud of stars. One talon held three arrows; the other an olive branch. The beak held a red banner trimmed in gold which read "U.S Infantry." On the back of the drum, written in fancy script, was the name *"Billy Young, 77th New York Infantry,"* followed by an impressive list of battles which included Harper's Ferry and Antietam.

Despite some nicks and scratches, the drum still had the luster of a new instrument. When the soldiers cleaned their guns, Billy cleaned his drum. His drum was his weapon. In his hands, it thundered like a cannon. If drumbeats were bullets, the war would have ended months ago with a Union victory. General Young and his top notch staff of drummer boys would have signed the surrender document and been hailed as the nation's heroes.

Moses returned the drum then picked up his own. Despite its battered and bruised looks, it still had a crisp and clear sound. The drumheads were serviceable, and the shell was free of cracks or splits. Any markings on the exterior had been covered under layers of grit and grime. The drum had been at his side since his induction with the 97th Colored Infantry. He often joked with Billy that his drum had more miles than drumbeats. Placing the drum on the ground, he leaned back against his knapsack and folded his hands behind his head. He gazed at the stars and thought about home.

Despite being surrounded by thousands of soldiers and his best friend, he was lonely. Perhaps, his father had been wrong in allowing him to enlist. Maybe, he wasn't man enough for the army, or maybe he was too scared about tomorrow's battle. He feared he would throw down his drum and run in the other direction when it came time to face the enemy, a fate worse than death. Maybe, Captain Brookes was right. On second thought, he should stay in the rear.

To ease his troubled mind, Moses concentrated on other great mysteries in his life. It was a pleasant diversion which beat counting sheep. As he drifted off to sleep, the words of his grandmother filled his mind. What could be the family secret his grandmother mentioned, he wondered. His grandfather often told him adventure stories about Indians who once lived on the land, but certainly that was no secret. On other days, his grandfather played games, teaching him how to hear and feel sounds while blind-folded. Little Moses seemed to have a knack for it. His grandfather talked about being one with the forces of the universe whenever they played. Moses didn't quite understand all of it, but surely, that couldn't be a family secret. After he thought about it for a while, there really wasn't too much he knew about the man.

Da-rum! Dum-dum! Dum-dum! Dum! The next morning Billy and Moses sounded reveille. After breakfast, Captain Brookes ad-dressed the men. They were ordered to take a defensive position on the ridge in support of the 71st and 72nd Pennsylvania Infan-try and deploy as necessary.

"Sound the march," the first sergeant bellowed. The drum-mers pounded out the command. With the band leading the way, the two columns stepped briskly to the tune of "Yankee Doodle Dandy."

The ridge was a ribbon of blue as Union soldiers readied their positions. In the fields, burial details were still collecting bodies. Wagons were piled high with the dead. No officer wanted his men to see such a sight, but there were simply too many bodies. Morn-ing slowly melted into afternoon. All was quiet on the front. No one dared to even swat a fly for fear of attracting a sniper. Finally, after an eternity of waiting, someone made a move. Across the valley, cannons were pulled from behind the trees and wheeled into position. Slowly but surely, the pieces of the Confederate battle plan were falling into place.

The Yanks took notice but their immediate concerns were elsewhere. Men were tired and hungry from doing nothing. After hours on the front line, food and water were priorities. Even the appearance of General George G. Meade, the newly appointed commander of the Army of the Potomac, failed to rally sagging spirits. The men joked it would have been better if he had been driving a supply wagon.

"Come on, Moses. Captain said we could leave the line for a break," Billy chirped. "Things might be looking up. Just heard General George Custer has whipped Jeb Stuart behind the ridge."

"Imagine that," Moses chuckled. "Old red beard and young golden locks riding tall in the saddle and charging each other with sabers. Do you think that's the attack the captain was talking about?"

"I sure hope so. Everyone is getting edgy from being on the ridge."

Back in camp, soldiers wandered in small groups and talked. After hours on their stomachs, they welcomed the chance to stretch their legs and grab a cup of coffee.

"Incoming! Everyone down," a soldier screamed. A rush of whistling wind soared overhead.

Boom! Boom-Boom! Shells exploded everywhere. Hot shrapnel cut a deadly path. Men fell dead where they stood, many with canteens in their hands and pipes in their mouths.

"We've got to get back to the ridge," Billy yelled as he ran over and grabbed Moses by the arm.

The boys scrambled up the hill, falling flat on their faces at the sound of each explosion. They dove head first into a shallow trench just behind the crest and buried their heads in their hands.

"The drums," Billy shouted, rushing to his feet. "Save the drums." He sprinted forward and in one swoop reached down and grabbed a drum in each hand. He turned on a dime and raced back to the trench, sliding in feet first.

"Not a scratch on any of us," he said as he tossed Moses his drum. "With those moves, General Doubleday should let me play on his baseball team," he laughed.

Artillery fire now erupted from both sides. The cannonade pounded the earth like giant fists, tearing and ripping the sod. Union gunners, outnumbered two to one, matched the Confederates round for round. At the rate of fire, both ridges would be reduced to ant hills by the end of the day. The duel continued for hours.

"They need someone to fetch water," Billy yelled to Moses as they hugged the ground. "I don't know about you but I'm tired of being a groundhog."

It didn't take Moses long to reach the same conclusion. Rebel gunners had finally targeted the ridge and were landing shells with pinpoint accuracy. Now, the safest place was behind the ridge. Besides, Billy was a good luck charm, Moses reasoned. It was sound advice to follow your luck. "Count me in," he replied.

"Canteens filled here," Billy shouted, waving his cap over his head. Minutes later, the trench was filled with an assortment of wood and metal containers.

"Well, that part of the plan worked perfectly." Moses chuckled. "Now, what do we do with all these canteens?"

"Carry as many as you can and follow me. Run exactly where I run and fall exactly where I fall. I think I have the rounds timed. Ready?"

"Whenever you are."

"Go!" Billy yelled. "Run for your life!"

They dashed from the trench and ran towards General Meade's headquarters. The small farmhouse, a couple hundred yards behind the ridge, was in shambles. Windows and doors were smashed. Dead horses littered the yard. Unknowingly, Confederate gunners almost won the battle by mistake. Their errant shots could have wiped out the entire Union command. The battle would have ended before it began.

About a quarter of a mile past the house, Moses and Billy found the spring. At this battlefield oasis, the water spouted clear and cold into a small sandy basin. They cupped their hands and took a long drink before filling the canteens. When they were done, each had about twenty canteens dangling from the shoulders.

"I feel like an army mule. It's going to be a long run up that hill," Moses said with a distressed look.

"Don't worry. We'll be heroes. The men will treat this water like it's Pennsylvania whiskey. Yes sir, this stuff is fine sipping water," Billy replied confidently.

They sprinted up the hill with Billy in the lead. Kaboom! A volcanic explosion shook the ground like an earthquake. Both boys were slammed to the ground. Moses slowly rose to his hands and knees. Billy was still flat on his stomach.

"Come on, Billy! Get up," Moses yelled. He crawled over to Billy and rolled him over. His eyes were wide open. Blood trickled from his nose and ears.

"You can't die, Billy. Damn you," Moses screamed as he gently cradled the body in his arms. Tears streamed down his face and streaked the black dust on Billy's cheeks.

Moses wobbled to his feet. His ears rang and his head ached. He spun around and fell to the ground every time he tried to take a step. The concussion of the blast left him dazed and confused.

"Up the hill! Billy says up the hill," Moses muttered incoherently as he crawled to the top of the ridge. He fell into a trench totally exhausted. Soldiers scurried over his body to retrieve their canteens.

In a few minutes, he was back on his feet. Still weak and woozy, he decided to walk the ridge. "Billy Yank! Where are you Billy?" he cried out. Billy couldn't be dead, he reasoned. There were no shrapnel or bullet wounds. The shell merely knocked him unconscious for a few minutes. Right now, Billy was probably on the ridge looking for him.

About twenty feet from the trench, Moses saw Billy's drum. That was a good sign. Any place you found Billy's drum, you found Billy. In the scramble for the canteens, it must have gotten pushed aside. He hurried to retrieve it.

Kaboom! The drum disappeared in a shower of flames. When the smoke cleared, all that remained were a few slats of smoldering wood. Moses staggered back to the trench and collapsed. He covered his ears and closed his eyes. He didn't want to hear or see anymore of the army. He wished the war would go away forever.

Late in the afternoon, the shelling stopped. Moses slowly raised his head. The ringing in his ears and the blinding headache were gone. He felt refreshed as if he had just awakened from a good's night sleep. He took a few sips of water to clear his throat. He knew where he was and what happened. Billy was dead, and nothing was going to bring him back. Any minute, the attack would begin. There was no place to run and hide. There was no Billy to lean on. Little Moses was ready to meet his fate like a warrior.

Brushing the dirt from his uniform, he walked to the front of the ridge. The ground was littered with soldiers, horses, and pieces of regimental flags. The artillery took its toll. Many of the caissons and guns had been blown apart. With a lull in the action, gun crews, their arms and faces covered in black soot, worked frantically to restock ammunition and salvage the wrecks. Meanwhile, the first sergeant and the captain gathered up the company. The musicians were ordered to report to the rear. Moses wasn't giving up so easily.

"Sir, yesterday, you said I could stay on the ridge," Moses implored.

"That I did private, but things have taken a turn for the worse. The doctors need help with the wounded.

"But, sir, you said I earned the right to decide my fate. I've respectfully request you allow me to remain right here."

"Very well, Private Freeman," the captain said reluctantly. "The choice is yours. Do you want to stay on the ridge or report to the field hospital?"

"I'll stay," he responded confidently.

"Very well. You and Billy can join the left flank. I think it may be the safest place."

"Billy's dead, sir," Moses said mournfully.

The captain paused and cast his eyes to the ground. "If you still wish to remain, you may stay with me. I can always put a good drummer to use."

"Yes, sir," Moses said as a broad smile creased his face.

As Union soldiers stared across the valley, a line of brown and gray uniforms emerged from behind the trees. Like an army of ghosts, a great wave of soldiers moved silently across the open field. Led by the blue flags of Virginia, twelve thousand men marched shoulder to shoulder, row after row. The Yanks stood quietly and admired the precision of the undisciplined Rebs.

The attackers moved at a deliberate route step, covering about a hundred yards in a minute. As the line surged closer, the alert was sounded. Da-rum! Da-rum-dum-dum! Dum-dum! Moses pounded out the command with a fury. His drumsticks thundered.

Union artillery opened fire. Dead men catapulted in every direction. On signal, two thousand Union rifles cracked the air simultaneously, knocking down row after row of men. The Confederates continued to march, undeterred by the thinning ranks. Above the noise, they gave a blood curdling yell. They were doomed but not yet defeated.

Against all odds, the Rebels crested the ridge and broke the center of the Union line. Soldiers stood toe to toe, thrusting bayonets and firing rifles at point blank range. Screams and curses filled the air as men fell to the ground gasping for one last breath. Ghastly heaps of armless, legless, and headless corpses covered the ground. The blood on Cemetery Ridge flowed like a raging river.

An impossible victory was at hand. If the Confederates could fill the gap and turn the flanks, the Union army was in danger of being overrun. Captain Brookes watched nervously as enemy soldiers poured through the opening. He anxiously awaited for the order to counterattack. There was none. When the Rebs seized an artillery piece and aimed it down the Union line, he took charge. There was no time to wait. Seconds cost lives. Minutes could cost the battle. Standing upright, he waved his saber above his head. In a passionate plea, he challenged his men to battle.

"The Union must prevail. Who will follow me to victory?" he asked boldly. Frightened soldiers jumped from their hiding places and followed. It was their turn to dance with the devil, and they knew it. As they slowly beat back the attack, Moses found himself in the center of the hellish nightmare. His orders were to stay with Brookes, and he trailed behind him every inch of the way.

"Captain, behind you!" Moses yelled in terror. Before Brookes could respond, a Confederate soldier turned and pointed his rifle at Moses. The assassin squinted his eyes, clenched his teeth, and squeezed the trigger. Fire and smoke erupted from the barrel. Ker-rack! The minnie ball struck with the sound of lightning splitting a tree.

Moses grabbed his thigh. The pain was intense, worse than anything he had ever felt. He imagined his leg had been blown apart. As he tumbled backward, he saw the captain fire his pistol into the side of the man's head.

Moses landed on his back with his drum resting on his stomach. When he raised his hand to his face, it was covered with thick, dark red blood. He called out, but no words left his lips. Cries for help echoed down an endless cavern. His throat was parched and coated with dust. His body ached with a burning fever. Sweat poured from his face and stung his eyes. Looking up through a haze, he watched men beat each other to the ground with rifles, sabers and fists. Unable to move his legs, he feared being buried alive under a mountain of dead men.

"Only a bad dream," he mumbled over and over. Any second he expected to awaken and find himself back home in Hope

Springs. This carnage was too unbelievable to be true, he reasoned. Therefore, it must be a dream. Gradually, he began to relax. He closed his eyes and took a couple of deep breaths. The
pain eased. A cool breeze caressed his face. His skin tingled. His
body floated above the ground. He was being carried home. His
prayers had been answered. All of this was just a dream.

Moses found himself standing on the shore of a dark blue
lake. The air was still. The lake was as smooth as glass. In the
distance, a black eagle with a snow-white crown and a bright gold
beak circled the sky. Suddenly, the bird dove and splashed the
water. It struggled to gain altitude. Something clenched in its talons was weighing it down. The eagle flapped its wings furiously.
Passing overhead, it opened its talons and soared to the sun. Moving closer and closer to the fiery glow, the eagle dipped its wings
and vanished like an exploding star.

Moses stared at the sky. A strange object floated to the ground
and landed upright in the sand. From the colors and markings, it
looked like Billy's drum. When he stepped forward, he was surprised to discover it was Billy's drum. It appeared to have been
freshly painted. There were strange words and an emblem on the
front. Reaching down, he touched the shell. A burst of brilliant
white light blinded him. The drum and the dream disappeared in
a flash.

"It's Moses. He's still alive," called out the orderly, pulling
back the bloody sheet. "I thought he was supposed to be with
us."

"Looks like his leg is shot up pretty bad. Think we should
take him inside?" asked the other.

"You know what the doc said. Yanks first, civilians second,
Rebs third, and then anybody else. He doesn't want any Negroes
on his operating table."

"We've got to do something. He's one of us. Stay with him.
I'm going to get help."

Moses heard the voices but was too weak to respond. He was
locked in a dark tomb. "I must tell them I'm alive, but I can't even
move my lips," he screamed silently. A chilling thought crossed
his mind. He might be dead and waiting for his final judgment.
He imagined heaven with lush, green pastures and snowcapped

mountains. On the other side of the rocky peaks, he saw a bottomless pit with flames shooting wildly into the air as bodies were tossed into the inferno. With the long line of rebels waiting to see the devil, he might be able to sneak out of line himself.

The next voice Moses heard was soft and soothing. It reminded him of his mother. "You'll be all right, child. I'm going to take you inside."

The hospital tent reeked of chloroform. Moses felt pressure on his thigh as a bandage was applied. The slightest touch of his leg hurt, but he was happy for the pain. "I'm alive. I can feel," he cried out joyously in his mind. He raised his eyelids ever so slightly and stared at the white canvas ceiling. "But then if I'm alive, none of this is a dream," he sobbed. He closed his eyes and pictured his family. He would give anything in the world to be home. He promised himself he would never leave again. He had seen enough of the world to last a lifetime.

Thunder rumbled in the distance as a storm approached. Minutes later, the rain, whipped by the strong wind, crashed against the tent. The sound was like that of a thousand drummers, pounding out a frenzied beat. It was the sound of a street festival, a celebration of life.

Moses inhaled the fresh air and said a prayer of thanks. Today was the Fourth of July. For now, the killing had stopped. After three days of fighting, the armies had run out of bodies. Certainly, the gods of war were satisfied with the death and destruction.

Back in Hope Springs, Henry danced merrily in his field amid the mud puddles. The rain had saved the crop and the farm.

Chapter Eighteen—

Uncle Abe's Honor Guard

Moses was alive and fighting for his life. The soft-lead bullet missed the bone but flattened out to gouge a hole the size of a fifty-cent piece. The bullet and other dirty fragments were still in his leg. As the wound became infected, a deadly fever gripped his body.

From the moment the bullet struck, time had stopped like a broken watch. There were no mornings, afternoons or evenings, only an eternity of agony. Moses thrashed violently in his cot. One minute his teeth chattered from a bone-numbing chill. The next minute he tore at his clothes as a hot sweat drenched his uniform.

His mind wandered in a maze of pain. He was hopelessly lost in his own thoughts. Every corner he turned, he came face to face with his assassin. Somehow, he needed to forget the war and pull his thoughts in the other direction. He remembered a Bible story about a place called purgatory where sinful souls were cleansed by fire before entering into heaven. Surely, he was in purgatory or hell. His body continued to burn.

But why me, he thought, trying to remember his sins of the past. Every answer came back to the war. He was a drummer boy who had never even fired a rifle in anger; yet he volunteered to participate in this slaughter. The only answer was this unholy war. Brother killing brother over who owned another was the only sin for which he could be accountable. After all, he was a soldier in the army of man, not God. God must have decreed this war a more grievous sin than slavery. That's why he was being punished. The logic to God's reasoning was beyond the intellect of man.

Throughout the night, patients sobbed for their mothers. In the morning hours, their cries reached a crescendo. The Grim Reaper heard every word of these forlorn souls as he made his appointed rounds. He was a compassionate businessman. Those who cried out the loudest were the first ones scratched from his ledger.

Moses was no different than his comrades. In the early hours, the fever squeezed his body like a vise. "Opatunji, I will save you," he wailed one moment. "Opatunji, save me," he begged deliriously the next.

His mad ravings were largely unnoticed. They merely mingled with the other tormented voices in a choir of the damned, but someone was watching over him. Just when it seemed his body would explode from the fever, he felt a cold compress against his head or a spoonful of water pressed to his lips.

"No doctor, you're not going to cut the boy's leg off. Not after you left him here to die," said the woman in anger. Moses, still too weak to raise his head, recognized the voice. It was the woman he heard outside the tent.

"That's the prescribed treatment for this type of injury," the surgeon replied, standing with his surgical knife at the ready. "I don't have time to argue with you. There are hundreds of patients who need my attention. I'll take the bullet and leave the leg if you take him with you, but I warn you, he'll be dead in a few days."

Three days later, Moses awoke from his nightmare. The fever had broken. As the soft, warm hands massaged his face, he fully opened his eyes for the first time in a week. He tried to smile, but his body was stiff and sore from his head to his toes. His thigh still ached with a dull pain. He considered it a good sign until he remembered how the old-timers talked about the phantom. It wasn't uncommon for an amputee to feel pain for months or years after the limb had been removed. The thought scared Moses to death. He started to perspire profusely. Deliberately, he slid his hand along his side. "Whew!" he sighed with relief. The leg had been saved. The pain was real.

"Good morning, my name is Sarah Hummel, and you are a guest in my home," said the woman sitting next to his bed. With her alabaster skin and white apron, she looked like an angel. For a brief second, Moses thought that maybe he was in heaven.

"Moses Freeman is the name, but most people call me Little Mo. I want to thank you for saving my life," he said graciously. "I owe you a great debt."

"No," Sarah interrupted. "I'm the one who owes the debt. You risked your life for your country. It's the least I can do to repay my share."

"But why me?" Moses queried.

"My brother was killed at Antietam. He was only a child of eighteen. The day he died I vowed to look after the children of the war."

Moses looked around the parlor. The room was full of patients in their late teens or early twenties. "And what about your family?"

"My husband is fighting in the West, so I'm here alone. When the armies turned my farm into a cemetery, I turned my house into a hospital. I believe if I do good deeds here, God will bring back my husband alive. And what about your family? Night after night you called out for Opatunji."

Moses thought hard about the name. He didn't recognize it. "Must be something I heard from the men," he offered. "With the fever, I couldn't think very clear, but I do remember having strange dreams. I saw men fly like eagles."

Moses spent the next two months at the Hummel house. Recovery was slow and painful, but Sarah always provided a helping hand. When he was able to walk with a crutch, he was assigned as an orderly to Camp Letterman, the hospital built at the northern end of Gettysburg. During the day, he scrubbed floors, washed sheets and ran errands. In the evening, he performed his most important task. He took center stage as the ward reader. When the patients learned he could read, he was given an unofficial field promotion. For those few precious hours, he was known as "General Freeman" as a sign of their appreciation.

Every night he stood in the center of the room and read aloud. His oratory skills breathed life into the letters from home. His voice was strong and smooth. There was no stumbling over words. He fluctuated his tone for dramatic effect. In short, he read like an elder statesman and performed like a seasoned actor. To the men, it didn't matter if he was black or white, Rebel or Yankee. All that mattered was that Little Moses was educated.

"The name is Walter Davis with the 34th Virginia Volunteers," said the patient extending his hand. "I guess with all of these bandages covering my face, it doesn't matter what uniform I wore. The doctor said I should have my sight back in a couple of weeks, but until then, I was hoping you might read my letters."

"It would be my pleasure," replied Moses, sliding a chair next to the bed.

Every night for a week, Moses read to the sergeant. Afterwards, the conversation always drifted back home.

"Moses, if we lose this fight, my family will lose everything. My daddy has ten slaves working his farm. If they're freed, we're ruined."

"But that's what this war is all about, the end of slavery," Moses countered politely.

"I just don't know what you Yanks see in those Negroes. They're not people like you and me. They were born and bred to work in the fields."

"You've got to change your ways, Walter. They are people just like you and me. Give people a chance. I think you would be surprised how smart Negroes can be," Moses chuckled.

"Well, I don't think that will ever happen, but maybe, someday after the war, we can be friends. You seem like a real nice fellow."

"Maybe, someday we can be friends. But first, you have to get your sight restored," Moses replied. Secretly, he hoped he would be around to see the bandages removed. He prayed that Walter would finally see the light in more ways than one, but for the moment, the joke was too enjoyable to stop.

"Speaking of Negroes," Walter continued. "I heard your President Lincoln is speaking tomorrow at the cemetery."

"Now there's a man who knows something about the Negroes," Moses bellowed. "Maybe, you should hear what he has to say."

Early the next morning, Moses walked the hospital grounds and watched as the town busily prepared for the arrival of the President. Sidewalks were already crowded with visitors. A parade of carriages blocked traffic in an all directions. Local merchants warmly welcomed the army of politicians and bureaucrats from Washington. There were still mountains of battlefield souvenirs to be sold. In short, the dedication of the military cemetery had become a headline event which the sleepy town of Gettysburg had never witnessed.

Moses returned to his cot tucked away in a corner near the entrance and finished sewing the ripped seams on his uniform. If he was lucky enough, he might be able to sneak away for a few hours and listen to some of the speakers, and then if there was time, he hoped to find Billy's grave and lay a bouquet of flowers.

"Attention on the floor," a voice boomed as a group of high ranking officers lined the doorway.

"Put the men at ease," said one of the colonels. Moses stood at parade rest and stared in disbelief. Through the door stepped President Abraham Lincoln. He immediately recognized the Great Emancipator from pictures in the newspapers. His long, lean frame towered over everyone in the room. Dressed in a plain black suit with black boots, he looked more like a preacher than a president. His dark hair was slightly tousled in sharp contrast to his neatly trimmed beard. Deep creases lined his face like a crumpled piece of paper.

Mr. Lincoln briefly conferred with his staff, glanced around the room, and then walked down the center aisle. Stopping at each bed, he greeted patients with a kind word and a firm handshake. When he started down the other side, Moses froze with fear. Butterflies fluttered in his stomach. As the President drew near, his mouth dried up and his throat tightened. His knees wobbled. He tried to think of something to say, but there wasn't enough time.

Without moving a muscle, he strained his eyes to see the officers who walked with the President. To his surprise, one of them was Captain Brookes who wore the rank of major. The President greeted the last patient and headed toward Moses. Moses snapped to attention. Major Brookes stepped from behind the President.

"Mr. President," the major said. "This is the young soldier who saved my life."

The President extended his hand and smiled. "After hearing so much about you, it is, indeed, a pleasure to meet you. On behalf of the citizens of the United States, I commend you for your gallantry and would like the honor of presenting you with this award."

Major Brookes read the certificate. "Let it be known that Private Moses Freeman, Headquarters Company of the 77th New York Infantry, having distinguished himself in the service of the United States of America on the third day of July in the year of our Lord, eighteen hundred and sixty-three, at the Battle of Gettysburg, is hereby promoted to the rank of corporal. Given by my hand on November 19, 1863, Abraham Lincoln, President of the United States."

"A job well done, corporal. Your efforts to preserve the Union are greatly appreciated," the President said warmly as he handed Moses the certificate.

Moses beamed modestly. He scrambled for the right words to say. "Sir, the honor is mine. On behalf of my family, I want to thank you. You have given us the hope of freedom and we are eternally grateful."

The President smiled sheepishly and nodded his head. After he departed, Major Brookes remained behind.

"Here corporal," he said, handing Moses his new chevrons. "I think you'll be needing these before you leave."

"I wondered what happened to you after the battle. No one seemed to know anything," Moses said. "I thought I'd find your name on a headstone in the new cemetery."

"I survived without a scratch and received a promotion. My father pulled some strings to get me assigned to the War Department in Washington."

"I'll get my orders tomorrow when they start closing the hospital," Moses replied flatly. "Most likely, I'll be back in Washington, but I sure would like to find a unit heading south to Richmond."

Brookes ignored the request. "I have something else you'll find interesting. I was always fascinated about your grandfather, so I had my father do some research. In the records at Fort McHenry, he found the commander's journal. There was an entry from September 15th, 1814, which commended a drummer boy named Moses for saving the life of a sergeant. The boy was missing and presumed to have been killed in action. I don't know if that was your grandfather, but it's an odd coincidence. You did say your grandfather was killed in an accident."

"Doesn't appear to be the same person," Moses replied. "There were lots of slaves named Moses. Maybe, my grandfather was in a different battle."

"Anything's possible," Brookes reminded him as he got up to leave. "When you get to Washington, look me up. Oh, and one more thing. You should be receiving a package in the next day or two. Consider it a token of my appreciation for saving my life."

Saturday morning Moses returned from his errands. The package was setting on his cot. "Fragile-Musical Instrument" in bold letters was stenciled on the side. Moses carefully opened the box. Inside was a receipt from the Union Manufacturing Company in Baltimore, Maryland for "general cleaning and restoration." Moses pulled the drum from the box and gazed in amazement. His old parade drum had been magically transformed into the most magnificent drum he had ever seen, even better than Billy Yank's. No longer was this the battered drum given to him by his grandmother.

On the front of the drum was a black eagle with the words "Fort McHenry, Maryland 1814" painted in fancy scroll beneath its talons. Moses rubbed his fingers over the black eagle. He was hypnotized by the sight. It was the same eagle he had seen in his dream.

Holding the drum at eye level for a closer look, he noticed light penetrating through holes on opposite sides just below the top counterhoop. "Bullet holes," he mused as he stuck his finger into one of the holes. He lowered the drum to his hip. The bullet holes lined up perfectly with his thigh. "You saved my life. You do have the power of the universe," he said as lifted the drum to his face.

Peering through the holes, he noticed writing on the inside of the shell. His curiosity immediately got the best of him. He disassembled the drum and made a startling discovery. Someone had carved an inscription into the wood and then wiped it with ink. The ink seeped into the letters leaving a permanent record. Moses read the words over and over.

This drum is the spirit of all men bound by slavery. Its history extends from Africa to America. Whoever plays this drum shall sound the call for freedom. Fear not, Opatunji walks at your side.

Moses of the Chesapeake. Master Drummer, Hope Springs, Pennsylvania. October 1859.

Moses retrieved the receipt and slowly read it from top to bottom. It clearly stated cleaning and restoration. There was no mention of any paint or scroll work being done.

"So that was grandma's secret. Grandpa was a drummer at Fort McHenry," Moses uttered quietly with a sense of satisfaction. Major Brookes had been right about his grandfather.

"But what about the black eagle and Opatunji," he asked himself. There were more questions than solutions to this mystery. He had seen the eagle in his dream and called out to Opatunji, yet there was no explanation for either. Back home, his grandmother or father had the answers. Until then, he had no choice but to wait.

That evening, Moses carried the drum to the top of Cemetery Ridge where the Union soldiers halted the Confederate charge. He stood on the spot where he fell and lightly tapped on the drum. In the crisp and cold air, drumbeats floated across the barren wheat fields. The sound of Taps echoed to the far ridge where the Rebels had begun their fateful charge. The drum summoned the ghosts of the battlefield to assemble as brothers.

Chapter Nineteen—

The Legacy of the African Drummer

Orders were posted the next day. Much to his chagrin, Moses was reassigned to his original unit, the 21st United States Colored Troops at Fort Bennett, just across the Potomac River in Georgetown. While the Union army inched forward in the south, Moses found himself stuck in the mud of the nation's capital. Garrison life with "Uncle Abe's Honor Guard" was boring, especially to someone who considered himself a grizzled veteran. The only bright spot was the band. The chance to play with the regimental band was a welcomed interruption to the daily routine, but the music was not always a happy song.

After a few performances, Moses found the social scene to be irritating. While troops were starving, people in Washington were partying. There was always something to celebrate. Even with shortages of clothing and food at the front, civilian and military members of high society found time to dress in the finest costumes and dine lavishly. Then, there were the endless annoying questions from politicians and dignitaries about the black eagle on his drum.

Their fawning comments about the drum and a black drummer boy were humiliating. He had to get as far away from Washington as possible.

On New Year's Eve, Moses played at the officer's ball. While guests danced the night away, Moses fretted. After nearly a year on the music circuit, he was tired of the parties. He was a soldier, and a soldier belonged with the fighting army. He was also a black soldier assigned to a black unit. The only fighting he could expect was during payday card games. He had an escape plan, but it required perfect timing. Perhaps, tonight would be the time. Throughout the night, he searched the ballroom. Every officer in Washington was out there. Surely, Major Brookes was among them.

Minutes before the clock struck midnight, Moses spotted the major walking toward the bandstand with his date. His ticket out of Washington was right on time. All he needed was the right approach. He had done it at Gettysburg. He crossed his fingers; he could he do it again.

"Happy New Year, corporal," the major shouted as the crowd counted down to the new year.

"A Happy New Year to you, sir," Moses greeted the major. "Sir, I want to first thank you for the drum, but how did you know it belonged to my grandfather."

"I didn't know that," Brookes said in amazement. "I just picked up the drum on the battlefield and sent it away to be cleaned. Nothing more."

"I appreciate your generosity," Moses responded. Now was the chance to spring the trap. "While speaking of the new year, do you think you could get me a transfer? Be mindful, I appreciate all that you have done for me, but now I'm back to where I started. I don't want to end the war walking a guard post."

The major lowered the champagne glass from his lips and nodded his head in agreement. He knew Moses was calling in a favor.

"I know exactly how you feel. I'm a fighting man myself. Now all I do is battle bureaucrats. I wish I could go back to the front, but I'd step on too many important toes. I'll see what I can do for you. Many people say the war will end this year. It doesn't look like the Rebs can hold out too much longer."

Moses shrugged his shoulders. Brookes' answer was not encouraging. The major had his own problems. He didn't need anymore. Brookes and his date waltzed to the center of the floor as the clock struck twelve. Before disappearing into the dancers, he turned to Moses with a wink of an eye and a nod of a head. Moses smiled weakly. Maybe, he had a chance after all.

A week later, orders were announced at morning formation. Moses quietly cheered. He was assigned to a replacement battalion marching to Richmond. Before dismissing the formation, the company sergeant called him to the side.

"Good luck," he said sincerely. "We wish we could go with you. Just remember where you came from. Now you go and do your old regiment proud."

"I'll never forget my roots, sarge," Moses replied as he held up his drum for inspection. Painted on the shell in a unit banner next to the "77th Pennsylvania Infantry" were the words "21st U.S. Colored Troops."

The sergeant patted Moses on the back and grinned. "You've already done us proud. Now go and make someone else proud." Moses took one last look at his unit. He felt guilty. Standing at attention were rows of black soldiers who would gladly trade places. He was living their dream, and he knew it. This was not the time to simply walk away. They had to know they were part of the dream. He marched to the front of the formation and walked down the line. Stopping in front of each soldier, he snapped a crisp salute and rendered a firm handshake. This was the way for a soldier to say good-bye.

In February, Moses found himself in ankle-deep mud on the outskirts of Petersburg. He was cold and wet but it was a good feeling. He was standing on a battlefield only eight miles south of Richmond, the capital of the Confederacy.

For the first time in his career, Moses was assigned to a black infantry unit. They were the advance element. Their mission was to delay any attack with a hasty skirmish line. It was suicidal, but it was typical of the duties assigned to black units. Not a soul complained. They were ready for their baptism of fire. Fortunately, there were no Rebel attacks. The only battles were fought against insects, disease, the torrential rain, and the scorching sun. They claimed more casualties than the Confederates.

The great armies were locked in a stalemate. General Lee didn't have enough soldiers to mount an offensive, and General Grant didn't want to mount a high number of casualties. Major Brookes was wrong. The war wasn't coming to an end. It was simply stuck in the mud. Victory would go to the army which could dig the biggest hole. Both sides hunkered down in a maze of trenches which extended for miles. Shovels instead of rifles were the weapons of choice.

Finally, General Lee blinked. On March 25th, the stalemate was broken. Running low on supplies and high on desertions, the Confederates raced to the west to link with the rest of the army. Grant sent his cavalry around the flank to cut off the retreat. All infantry units were ordered to attack. The route of the Army of Northern Virginia had begun.

Da-rum! Dum-dum! Da-rum! Moses sounded the call as soldiers stormed over the trenches. For the next week, his regiment literally ran after the fleeing Confederates. They marched all day and all night, and begged for more. They had waited too long to be tired. They were eager to exact their revenge before a truce could be signed. They would march to hell and back without a drop of water if necessary. President Lincoln wanted the issue pressed, and no power on heaven or earth was going to stop them from pressing the enemy. Moses ran at the front of the column, pounding his drum with every ounce of strength.

The race ended on April 9th, 1865, at Appomattox Court House. There Lee met with Grant to sign the surrender documents. The colored regiments were more relieved than disappointed. Although they desperately wanted to slay their foe, they rejoiced. They thought the end of the war was the end of slavery. No greater victory could be won.

Three days later, Moses and his unit lined the road to the village as Confederate regiments surrendered their colors. Columns of gaunt and scraggly men, dressed in tattered gray and brown uniforms, marched down the lane. Arms were stacked and battle flags handed to Major General Joshua Chamberlain.

All was quiet. Not a word was spoken. No bugle blared or drum beat. Moses stood with his drum at his side. When the order was finally given to strike up the band, the musicians played a rousing version of "John Brown's Body."

After the ceremony, the Yanks marched back to camp. Moses hammered his drum to the rhythm of the shuffling feet. Despite standing at attention for hours, he felt energized. His body vibrated with the sound of the drum. He tingled with pride as the Negro units passed. Every face, young and old, wore a hardened and harried scowl. From the ragtag uniforms, it was obvious that many of these soldiers were liberated slaves. Today, they walked tall. In a few hours, they would be mustered out of service. They were going home as victorious soldiers, and no one could ever take that away.

Out of the corner of his eye, Moses noticed one of the soldiers. His eyes followed the man until he disappeared from sight. For some strange reason, he was drawn to this individual. Over the years, he had met hundreds of Negro soldiers. Surely, he must have seen this man somewhere before. He couldn't explain the attraction, but it was more than usual curiosity.

Moses stepped into the road. Could it possibly be, he thought. He called out, but the soldier did not hear him. "Grandpa! Grandpa!" he called again, running along the column.

Distracted by the shouts, the old soldier scanned the crowd to his left and right. The voice sent chills down his spine. Was that a ghost from the past? he asked himself. He continued marching. The voice called out again. This time he stopped and turned around. A young boy was running towards him. As the boy drew near, he saw the black eagle. The drum had finally returned. Drum and drummer were reunited.

"Moses, my Little Moses," the old man shouted joyously as he caught the boy in his arms. "It's a miracle!"

"No, Grandpa. You're the miracle. Everybody believed you had drowned," said Little Moses.

"I washed ashore. After a few days on the run, I was captured and sold down south," Big Moses recalled. "I didn't dare tell anyone I was at Harper's Ferry. I would have been shot for treason. When the Yanks freed me, I joined the army to get back home. Only this time, my enlistment was official. And how did you end up in Uncle Abe's army?"

"I convinced father to let me enlist. I don't know how to explain it, but a voice inside my head kept telling me to join."

After a long embrace, Moses set down his grandson and picked up the drum. "This drum is a powerful force, an instrument of the gods," he said, rubbing his hand over the maple shell. The sight of the black eagle brought back a flood of sweet memories. Patayac, Hart, Henry and Sergeant MacDonald came to mind for the first time in many years. Little Moses saw the wistful look in his grandfather's eyes.

"Then you are the black eagle?" he asked, hoping to answer one of the nagging questions from Gettysburg.

"No. I only saw the eagle in my dreams. Three times exactly. The last time was last summer, the night before I was freed."

"I saw the black eagle when I was wounded at Gettysburg," Little Moses declared. "It soared to the heavens and disappeared into the sun."

"A good omen. It means the spirit of Opatunji is free," Big Moses replied cheerfully with a big smile.

"Then you are Opatunji?" Little Moses asked, still confused.

"No. Opatunji was may grandfather, your great-great grand-father. He was a master drummer, a holy man from his village. He died in this country as a slave without his drum. For breaking the sacred bond between drum and drummer, he was condemned to walk the earth until someone proved worthy to free him. That person had to be another drummer."

Little Moses was startled by this revelation. "But weren't you the master drummer who consecrated the drum?"

"I only dedicated the drum for a righteous cause. I saw the magic in the drum but lost faith. I proved unworthy. It was your bravery that consecrated the drum."

"Then the mystery of the drum is the story of Opatunji?" Little Moses inquired.

"The story of Opatunji is the story of every man who seeks freedom. Until now, I never fully understood the mystery of the drum, but now it is clear. The spirit of Opatunji could never be free until his family was free. As long as his family was enslaved, he was trapped in the spirit world."

"Then the drum was the instrument of our freedom?"

"The drum and the drummer as one being was the liberator. When you saved the life of your captain, the drum saved yours. You proved to be the worthy successor to the master drummer. You restored the sacred bond, and the curse was lifted. You freed Opatunji to hear our prayers, and our prayers were answered."

"Now that the war is over, will we be free forever?"

"The torch of freedom has been passed down to your genera-tion. We will be free as long as you hold it high. The flame must never fade."

Big Moses placed the shoulder strap around his neck and turned the drum sideways. "Let us celebrate our victory like our forefathers. The spirit of the drum has come full circle."

Moses tapped lightly on the drum. Seconds later, his fingers danced across the drumhead like a thousand raindrops. The sound floated to the heavens. In the distance, an eagle glided over the valley, a black speck on the blue horizon.

About the Author

Paul J. Travers received a B.A. degree from the University of Maryland and a M.A. degree from Pepperdine University. He served in the U.S. Marine Corps as an amphibious armor officer.

A former historian for the Maryland Park Service, Paul is the author of *The Patapsco: Baltimore's River of History and Eyewitness to Infamy.*

Currently, he serves as a historical consultant to the Maryland Historical Society and local museums and preservation groups.